Still Standing
After the Bell

Wm. Brent Hensley

12-8-18

ISBN:10:1533375089
ISBN-13:978-1533375087

DEDICATION

This book is dedicated to my mother, Evelyn Hensley Payne who grew up in the boxing family on which this story was based. She learned priceless life lessons through the sport of boxing and the men in it. Her stories and tales of boxing gave fuel to the idea to write <u>Still Standing</u>. She was in her own way a fighter her whole life, and she instilled this quality of fighting spirit in all her children.

Brent Hensley

Chapters

Still Standing

By Wm. Brent Hensley

Forward

This is a story of small town boxing shown through the eyes of a unique young man, a prizefighter, who throughout his life learns to deal with adversity and the ability to endure at great odds. The story starts in the era of World War II, around the last few months of the war, but follows him through the ebbs and flows of his exceptional life. Based on the horrors of war, this story shows how the new modern war brought with it not only all types of modern killing equipment, but along with new weapons, came new medicines with state of the art hospital care on the front lines. This would be the first war that would put those two technologies at odds with each other and on a scale like never seen before. So now you have more survivors dealing with a different type of suffering that will last long after the war has ended. Man will always invent new ways to kill and maim but hopefully mankind will always find new ways to climb out of that hell of suffering and endure. This is that story....

Chapter 1

Entering the Unknown

IT WAS JUST ANOTHER SUMMER NIGHT on patrol as a dozen of U.S. Army soldiers were working their way down a small dirt road just pass a farm house in the dark of night. Tensions were high. Everyone seemed to know the enemy had to be in the area, all the recon showed this was the case and the men in this patrol knew it as well. Half the men were still hung-over getting in from a weekend of fun, the first of which they had seen in months. The others were exhausted from the reconnaissance night after night and these few had been on patrol for three straight nights. Regardless of their condition they were ordered out on patrol once again. Headquarters knew the Germans did not want to leave Sicily defeated and holding this land just outside of Palermo was a must for Hitler's plan for Italy to work. And the Allies could not afford to relinquish the land they fought so hard for.

The air was still, not a breath of air was moving, and the moon was on the rise as it made faint shadows of men on the road. The area of road they were approaching was very narrow at this point; the olive trees and foliage seemed to be extremely thick and dense on both sides of the dirt road. Not normal landscape for this rocky and dry patch of earth of Sicily. The only noise to be heard was the rustling of equipment strapped to their backs and that of a dog barking in the distance. Suddenly the patrol of men seemed to stop and stand still on the road as if they were frozen, watching the glow of a light in the distance. It looked as if the sun was rising. The dark night sky lit up as if it was daytime, the glowing flare giving away the Americans' position, as all hell broke loose.

"Cover, take cover," was shouted out as the soldiers ran for cover and returned fire at the unknown.

Gunfire rang out all around the patrol and it seemed to be coming from all directions as the groves of olive trees lit up from gun fire. Several men were cut down right in the middle of the road. Others tried to make their way to the tree line just feet from the roadway, where they too were mowed down like fresh grass by machine gun and rifle fire.

"I've got to get out of here," raced through Pete's mind as he struggled on which direction to go. "But where?" he thought as he lay flat on his back on the road trying to be invisible. His eyes were blinded once again as the sky lit up from another flare. As his eyes adjusted he saw his way out.

"Hey over here," someone shouted as another soldier saw the opening as well. It was through a cornfield on the other side of the road. They waited as the flare faded out and dark surrounded them once again. Pete then jumped up and left his position on the road, heading toward freedom and away from the ambush, he thought.

Once again gunfire was heard, much closer to him. Pete ran for his life, while the machine guns firing bullets whizzed over his head. He heard the cries of other men as they too were hit and cut down by the gunfire. Pete kept running without looking back, in a zigzagging pattern, hoping to avoid being hit as he ran for cover in the cornfield. Once he made it there he realized he was all alone, after being torn from his regiment through the chaos of bombs, gunfire and total darkness. His heart was pounding, and with every step he took, it was one of uncertainty. His feet twisted and turned with every rock and dirt clog he stepped on from the freshly plowed ground.

It never dawned on him that part of the field was full of tall corn stalks and other parts had just been recently plowed ground. He just kept running like a spooked horse. As he ran he kept bobbing up and down in hopes that the bullets would miss. Further and further he worked his way from the road and far from gunfire. He could hear the battle faintly in the distance and at this point he felt pretty confident that he had out foxed his adversary. He slowed his pace to a fast walk, and slowly he got to a point where he stopped and turned just to scout out his position and to catch his breath. Pete looked up at the beautiful sight of the full moon and thought for a second of back home and how that same moon was the one his mother could be watching right now. There was no thought of war. For that one second, he let his guard down, allowing his mind to think of a more peaceful feeling, like being in his woods back home. And that was what he was thinking just before his life changed forever. He then took one more step.

Like being hit by a slugging heavy weight fighter, Pete was cut down off his feet. It was a flash... the explosion slammed him to the earth with a heavy blow like he had never taken in the ring before. The deafening explosion sent him into a world of drunken mayhem, causing him not to understand anything that had just taken place. He lay there on his side like a junky in Central Park, mouth and eyes wide open and his brain numb to reality, while the war was going on all around him. And then silence. His world turned to pitch black darkness.

Hours or perhaps days had passed...How much he does not know... He lay there slowly regaining his senses and thinking what the hell had just happened. The quiet was deafening.... No bombs, no guns, just a muffle ringing noise in his pounding head as he watched his breath in the dark, cool air. He could see the flash of gunfire and the lights of battle in a distance, but no noise... just a sharp ringing noise in his ears and pain was replacing the numbness, as it took over his entire body. Plus all kinds of thoughts raced through his mind. Where the hell was Sleepy, Speedy and the rest of his boys? I wasn't supposed to be even on that patrol. And how the hell could I have gone from drinking, girls and fun times in one minute to laying on my back in an open field of the damned, in the next? The pain started to hit him again in waves to the point of being unbearable and he fell back into an unconscious state. He would awake for periods of time, a minute or two here and there as his mind would come and go. This scenario would repeat itself for hours as he remained in this drunken like state.

Chapter 2

Party Boy

 THE CAPITAL CITY OF PALERMO, SICILY was full of life as the wine and beer flowed. There was no thought of war on those boys' minds. The hell with Patton, right now, this minute, was all they were thinking about... the enjoyment of wine, women and song, as the band played to the sounds of the big bands like Woody Herman and Glenn Miller. Cigarette smoke and noise filled the air of the dance hall at the USO club. Pete's year had started as a grocery wholesaler dealing in staple foods and stuffing bags for old women. That is, till he got the call from Uncle Sam that he had been selected by his friends and neighbors to serve in the U.S. Army. He vowed right then and there not to have anything to do with a so called friend or neighbor ever again. It wasn't of *if* he was going to the Army but *when*. Nevertheless, getting the news on Christmas Eve sucked.

   "Get your ass up old man," said Sleepy Johnson, as he kicked the back of Pete's chair.

   Pete was slumped over the table about half drunk. Sleepy and Pete were old buddies that grew up together back home in a little back water crossroad of a town in Hopedale, North Carolina. Somehow they lucked up and were shipped out together. After all, they were the best of friends their whole life and being in the same outfit was just fine to these two. Sleepy was about five foot nothing, bald headed, drowsy - eyed and maybe a hundred pounds, and always seemed to have a cigar wedged in the corner of his mouth. Pete was a large man, dark wavy hair, a good looking fellow, over six feet tall with a big heart and big hands. He was a heavy weight boxer on the weekends, and Sleepy was his corner man…. before Uncle Sam got in the way. They were two peas in a pod… whenever Sleepy got in trouble, which was more often than not, Pete was there. And lucky for most folks, Pete's size alone often would back a lot of people down. They were running buddies in life and now in war, which had ran them both all the way to Sicily.

They had been having a big night on the town when the two got separated. Sleepy was looking for Pete for hours. He had hooked up with two girls, Lisa and Betty. He told them both about his friend Pete and they were both dying to meet him. Sleepy was thinking about where in the world was Pete as he walked back in to the USO Club. As he looked in the corner at the back of the club he spotted his pal, dead drunk with a smile on his face.

"Wake up you old fart," Sleepy ordered his friend. Pete started to move and Sleepy shook him pretty hard and called for him to wake up once more.

As Pete came to he shouted, "Shut up Sleepy! Can't you see I'm talking to a lady here?"

"A lady! Hell she's drunker than you and passed out to boot," said Sleepy. "And as far as I can tell she ain't too good looking either."

The girl he was talking about was face down in the plate of spaghetti that Pete had ordered for her hours ago! Too drunk to know better, Pete had been talking to her without interruption for about the same amount of time. "I can't get drunk enough to make her good looking, but I can drink till I'm blind," said Pete as he laughed. " But she's an awful good listener, and she seemed to understand me better than just about anyone I know."

"Come on friend before Patton and the war catches up with us," said Sleepy as he helped Pete to his feet. "Look I got two babes waiting on us for tonight. Now don't you screw this up," Sleepy said, grinning and winking at Pete.

"Screw what up?" Pete said, as he tripped over his own feet, hitting the back of a couple of chairs, almost falling down in the process. "I know how to meet girls," he said as he tried to straighten up the crooked chairs. "You just walk up to them and say 'hey girl want to kiss'?" Pete laughed.

Sleepy stood there looking at Pete shaking his head, wondering how Pete got this drunk so fast. "Look partner you need to clear your head with some coffee or something," said Sleepy. "You need to go outside and get some fresh air and I'll go back and get the girls. We'll be waiting on you across the room at the front door."

"Ok Sleepy sounds good. I'll go get the girls a couple of drinks and meet you guys at that table across the way and will be right back. Night sunshine," Pete said as he patted the drunken girl on the back and she did not move. Pete slowly set sail on his way to the door as he tried to walk in a straight line.

"Ok, good luck," Sleepy shouted over the band as Pete studied on his conquest of the bar or fresh air, whichever would come first.

Chapter 3

Friday Night Fights

FRIDAY NIGHT FIGHTS at the old movie theater was packed with fight fans wanting to see their favorite home town star. You see, on Fridays town folks would turn the movie houses or Town Halls into a fight arena. In almost every little mill town and hamlet in the south Friday was fight night. These guys would put on a show traveling all over the state promoting themselves as the next Joe Louis or Jack Dempsey. The fight card would be a lot of the same names that you knew because they would fight as much as two or three times a month, not a year!

These were hard times for poor textile workers, farm hands, ditch diggers, shoe shiners, and any hardworking stiff. Boxing was their way out. They would travel together to save their money and would form teams, stables as they were, in places like Lou Kemp's Emporium Gym in Charlotte and Chick McCurry's place in Lincolnton, North Carolina. Weekly wages in those days were around ten to fifteen dollars. A guy working his way up on the fight card could get three to four times that much a fight. By day they worked like everyone else and on Friday nights they were local heroes. This was the so called farm system for boxing in the hay day of the sport. Days leading up to the fights you would see ad men walking around town wearing the fight cards on sandwich boards, with names like; Bob "Bobcat" Montgomery, Navy Bill Boyd, Sidney "Beau Jack" Walker, Jackie Nick Theodore, Maxie Shapiro, just to name a few. A lot of these fighters would come out of the Army, Navy, the Citadel in Charleston, or the Marine Corps. Charleston had two great trainers in both Woody Woodcock and Matty Matthews that would help young men at the Citadel hone their craft.

But wherever they came from, the road they traveled to get there was hard. There was no medical or workmen's compensation insurance, and if you were injured or hurt in the ring chances were good you would be out of work in your regular day job as well. No one had the money for heath care or their own doctor in their corner. Whichever doctor worked the fights that night would most likely be the only physician either boxer would see, regardless of the severity of his injuries. And no one thought of concussions in those days. The boxers got knocked out, that's all, no big deal.

They were tough and hard men, most without an education. After their fight career, the majority most likely fell back on hard times. Very few would make it and most of these pioneers are long forgotten. Being pro or amateur, Friday night in America in the nineteen thirties and forties was more than just a brawl between two men slugging it out. It was their only chance they had for what they thought could lead to a better life and maybe a little fame along the way.

And tonight was no exception, as both fighters for the main event, Pete Smith, "The Hopedale Homicidal" verses "Hard Rock" Harden, climbed through the ropes. The place was packed with serious fight fans to see what they knew would be a donnybrook of a fight. And in Pete's corner was Sleepy, on the ready to take care of his boy and best friend. They had been waiting months for this rematch, and they both just knew it had to go, this time in their favor. Everyone that had crowded in the State Theater sat or stood there as both excitement and smoke filled the air of anticipation for what was about to occur. The room lights dimmed as the ring lights focused on both men meeting in the center of the ring as the referee gave his final instructions. The two focused their stares straight through each other without a blink, as if they didn't hear a word the referee was saying. Both boxers were dancing and moving around as to be keeping the blood pumping in their legs and staying loose. Everyone in the crowd seemed to lean in as if they were receiving the instructions themselves. When the rules and instructions were over the boxers nodded their heads to the referee in agreement of what they just heard, and then hit each other's gloves as they broke to their prospective corners. They then received the last few words of strategy and encouragement from their handlers and removed their robes and donned their mouth pieces and stood there on the ready for the bell to sound and they waited. The bell rings.

Chapter 4

Back to the Unknown

THE DARK AND COLD WAS SETTING IN NOW on Pete….There was no gunfire, nor bombs exploding. They, too, had stopped. But the one constant had not was the ringing in his ears and the pain throughout his body! Pete came to realize he was alone in the dark in the middle of a cornfield. The understanding of what just happened had not reached his brain but it was slowly getting clearer. He remembered running then the flash of the explosion then nothing. He remembered being on patrol but he could not think of any of the names of men he was with. As he tried to rise up the intense pain had traveled all over his body. He just laid there in the mud, shouting.

   "Sleepy, Bill, Speedy, any of you guys out there?" No reply. Those were the names of his tank crew but it was the only names he could remember. He must have been out for hours he thought. There was no sign of life anywhere, just broken corn and bodies and surrounding him were large holes in the ground everywhere.

   "I must be in a damn mine field, "he thought. "How the hell did I do that and how do I get out of here?" This was racing through his mind, but all he was really thinking of was the pain…. "O' my God, why does it hurt so bad?" he thought. "Hell I'm a fighter I can handle pain," but this was nothing like anything before.

It had to be around dawn and Pete's eyes were finally clearing of dirt and mud, when he understood the situation was worse than he could ever believe. He used his left hands to feel where the pain was, because his right arm and leg was broken, he knew right off but his search then stopped abruptly, and then he suddenly understood. "O my God!" he thought. "My leg, O God, the damn thing is gone! O…. Jesus. Why me?" As he placed his left hand over his mouth as he cried out. And there was no blood. He felt down his leg one more time. Where the hell was the blood? There has to be blood if his leg was gone. "Shit, O' God……Damn," he shouted out but his cries did not help remove the pain, nor get attention from any bystander. There was no one.

All of this was going on in his mind in a flash. "The blast must have burned the skin and cauterized the wound. That had to be it," he thought as he inhaled the smell of burnt flesh. It was horrible. The leg and area around it was still smoking. Trying to be calm he prayed, "Please God, please help me to endure this," he demanded from both himself and God.

Still talking Pete said, "Ok it happened, calm your ass down, damn it. You were in a battle dumb ass, and now let's figure this out. Calm down and get your stuff together, like your gun. Where's your gun? Helmet, find your helmet. I got it. Be careful, you are in a mine field." Hearing is own words calmed himself a little.

So he kept talking to himself aloud and started ordering himself to toughen up. "Get your shit together. The leg is cauterized so you're not going to bleed to death, not soon anyway." His heart and mind were still racing but he was trained to deal with any tough situation. "But no one can train for this," he thought.

In those few seconds his world was turned upside down, full of confusion that would last for what would seem like years, as he started the waiting game for help. And still no noise, not a sound of life, just his own. Then in the distance a very faint sound of, "help me."

"Help…..me." Once again he thought he heard the cry for help. He laid there as quiet as he could, he tried so hard he was straining to block out the ringing noise in his ears long enough to hear the phantom cry for help.

"Could it be someone else in the same hell as I'm in?" he thought. Pete cried out, "Hey over here….. Hey over here, it's going to be ok, help is coming." Not knowing what to say or do, then listened again and wait a couple of seconds, than Pete repeated, "Hang in there buddy, help is coming." He waited again, as the seconds ticked by into minutes. It seem to Pete to be such a long time of silence, there was no sound from the voice in the distance. He relaxed back down in the mud, for there was no answer to his cry as he thought the worst.

Pete started checking on himself finishing his inventory and working on his own morale.

"You are still alive for now," he said, talking to himself and still organizing his gear and checking his ammo and weapon. "Yeah I'm good," he said as he finished his self inspection. He shouted once again, "Help is coming. Hang in there buddy." Still, he heard no reply. Pete waited and listened until he fell back into a deep sleep as the sun rose into the sky as the buzzards circled.

Chapter 5

The Hard Rock Fight

 THE BELL RANG the start of the first round and Pete was out of the corner like a shot.

   "Get'em boy," Sleepy said as he grabbed and pulled the stool back under the ropes. Left, left, left, right to the body, then a hard upper cut to the jaw and another left hook, right hook, and back to the body. Pete was hitting him with all he had and as fast as he could. After all, this was Hard Rock Harden, the heavy weight champion of both the Carolina's. On this night Pete was thinking how his life would change forever when he knocks out the champ. But it would have to be in the early rounds. No one had gone the distance with Hard Rock, six- two, two hundred and twenty five pounds of pure boxer with a chin like granite and a right hook like an anvil. Pete knew all too well about Rock Harden. This would be the third time they had battled and he hoped the outcome was not going to be the same as the last two.

   "But not this night, this night is mine," thought Pete. "I have trained too hard for tonight to be a rerun. I'm the home town kid, my folks, heck the whole town is with me on this night." Pete watched Rock's every move, trying to anticipate his next. After the opening barrage of hits from Pete, the two seemed to settle down to a slower and more cautious pace. The second round was more of the same, Pete driving in on Hard Rock, and Rock standing there taking everything Pete had to throw at him. Finally, in the fifth, Hard Rock broke out of that mold and started throwing some hard jabs and a few right crosses. Pete was thinking for a minute Rock had awaked but once again Rock went back on the defense and covered back up from Pete's assault. At this point Pete was trying to conserve his energy, and feeling pretty good of going the distance. He could not afford going at him on full assault mode like he did in the first few rounds. That truly would be foolish. After all, knocking out Hard Rock would be a straight up hard thing to do in Pete's mind.

Round after round Hard Rock again seemed to take everything Pete was throwing at him. Hard Rock would push Pete back, and then cover up, but for the most part he seemed to stand there, toe to toe with Pete and suck up every shot Pete had, and then in the eighth he started to make his move.

Sleepy with his towel draped around his neck, grabbed the corner stool and water pail, he then placed them in position as Pete made his way to the corner. Chewing on his cigar like gum, Sleepy quickly cooled off his boy with a wet sponge as he started on his litany of instructions.

"OK Bud, you are doing fine, keep doing what you're doing. Keep your hands up and jab, keep that in his face the whole time you hear me, and move, keep him off you, move your feet, I think he's getting tired, he is definitely getting tired," said Sleepy as he offered Pete some water and advice in the corner between rounds.

"Tired, hell he ain't moved, he hasn't moved the whole time. I'm the one dancing like Fred Astaire out there," Pete shouted.

"Now calm down Pete, and keep taking it to him," Sleepy explained. "He ain't all that. You keep that jab in his face and work on his body. You got him this time partner, keep it up." Pete shook his head in agreement, replaced his mouthpiece and stood up for the next round.

The bell rang to start the round; Pete was in his own world, fixed on offense and taking the fight to the Champion once again. They touched gloves and started back to what looked like a repeat of the other seven rounds. Pete started to move his feet and jab like he was instructed and that's when Rock Harden threw a powerful punch, the thunderous right cross of Hard Rock Harden found its' mark. Pete walked right into it. Without warning Hard Rock's dangerous right blow found its target over Pete's left eye and temple. It was like the recoil from a howitzer. The looks on the faces of the town folks were frozen in awe when Pete's feet came off the canvas. Once again a left jab and the powerful right hook and the trajectory was a pin point shot from Hard Rock Harden taking Pete off his feet again. This time it was like watching in slow motion, as his body was laid out flat in midair. What a combination of shots the champ had landed! Pete's body came bounding to the canvas with a thud. The referee started his count. There was no need. And just like that it was over.

Sleepy was hovering over his boy. "Wake up Pete, sit up!" he commanded. It seemed like minutes had gone by when finally, Pete's eyes opened in a cloudy blur as he stared at the crowd of folk hovering over him.

"Y'all get back, back up can't you see he's trying to breathe," ordered Sleepy as he pushed back on the mob while checking on Pete the whole time. "They don't call the son of a bitch Hard Rock for nothing! Woo, what a shot! You are lucky to live through that one my boy." The crowd started to disperse as Pete slowly set up on the canvas trying to get his bearings, but still not clear on what had happened. The ringing in his head was loud enough to know the fight was over.

"Did I hurt him that bad?" Pete asked with a smile on his lips.

"Yep, you damn near crushed his feelings," Sleepy said as he helped his partner back to the corner stool.

"You OK?" said the slow, deep voice of Hard Rock Harden, as he checked on the condition of his opponent.

"See ,"said Sleepy. "You damn near killed his personality, "as he made fun of his slow southern drawl.

"Yes sir I think I'm fine. Thanks Rock. We are ok," Pete said as they both tried to laugh it off.

"Let's go home partner. There ain't anything going on here. This night is over," said Pete, as they both got to their feet. The crowd was still shouting Hard Rock's name as Pete and Sleepy limped their way out of the ring to the locker room and then back home from a tough Friday

Chapter 6

Patton's Men

THE INVASION of Sicily in the summer of forty three was named Operation Husky. It was the second largest amphibious landing of the war, which utilized every resource possible. The combined air and sea landings consisted of over one hundred and fifty thousand troops, four thousand aircraft and three thousand ships for a landing that took only a few days. But it was nearly cancelled due to weather. However, this too worked in favor of the Allies. The defenders would assume that no one would attempt a landing in such weather conditions, yet alone one of this size, and it worked. But to ensure that an assault of this magnitude would be a success, a second operation was conceived. The other operation coinciding with it was called Operation Mincemeat. Mincemeat was an elaborate scheme to fool the Germans, and was all together a phony invasion, meant as a planned diversion in making the Germans believe that the Allies were invading Greece, not the real target of Sicily. The plan was to use a British solder's corpse and dress him to appear as a British officer. They then set him adrift off the coast of Spain wearing handcuffs which were attached to a briefcase full of intricate and detailed plans and so called, top secret documents. These included Allied ships and troop traffic, photographs and maps of the entire Greek and Mediterranean coastline region, even train schedules, and they were all a fake. The strategy worked, leaving Hitler to believe that reinforcing the coastline of Greece was not only smart, but the right thing to do. He believed so strongly in this divergent he had his number one field officer, Field Marshall, Erwin Rommel, the "Desert Fox", go to Greece himself. And even days into the battle Hitler continued to warn his officers to expect the main landing at Corsica or Sardinia. The result changed the course of the war. Hitler's belief caused the Germans to divert a large amount of their resources which included over half of their fleet of ships, men, tanks and supplies to Greece and making the real invasion of Sicily a much easier target to obtain.

Meanwhile, when all of this was going on the campaign was winding down as the fighting in North Africa was concluding. Pete and the gang found themselves, along with the rest of Patton's seventh Army, in Palermo, Sicily. The Allied Generals, Eisenhower and Alexander, were in command, and they thought to stage a cross-channel invasion, in lieu of an attack on France. Once everything was in place and operation Mincemeat was proved to be fully engaged, it was decided to invade Sicily with the goal of eliminating the island as an Axis base. This would certainly help open the sea lanes in the Mediterranean and would lead to the fall of Mussolini's government.

But the war Pete and Sleepy found themselves in was the war fought mostly between their General, Patton, and the leader of the British forces, General Bernard Montgomery. Those two hated each other and the race to the port of Messina was on. You never got tired of where you were because you would not be there long enough to grow bored. The invasion was in two places, Montgomery's eighth army from the eastern side of the island in Task Force 545 and Patton's seventh army arrival was from the west in Task Force 343. They both supposedly reported to British General Sir Harold Alexander who was in charge of the fifteenth Army Group. But every time Patton felt as though Monty was getting the upper hand, Patton once again would put the seventh army back on the track to Messina, and it felt as if they had been on the move for months. That was the life under Patton, move, hold and advance. All through North Africa and now Sicily, Patton was always racing to beat Monty to the finish line. Wherever Eisenhower drew the line in the sand Patton made sure he was there first, and the hell with his men. They all thought at times, it was all about being first at all costs.

Palermo was where Patton got in trouble slapping that kid in the hospital for what Patton's view of him was that of being a coward. Pete and the guys never forgot it. General Eisenhower made Patton stop his advance and apologize to all his troops. Because of that incident the 7th Army got to slow down and rest in Palermo a few weeks more than Patton hoped. "I wish that son of a bitch would slap me," one would guess they all thought. One sure thing about General George Patton, he always wanted his men to fear him more than the enemy. And it worked most of the time.

With smoke pouring out of the mess tent, the smell of fresh cooked Bar B-Q was in the air, as the two officers made their way inside the tent. "Attention," someone cried out and there, standing in the opening of the mess tent, was old 'blood and guts' himself, General George S. Patton. Pete and Sleepy could not believe their eyes and neither could everyone else in the mess tent as they jumped to their feet in response to the order of attention given.

"Keep your seats," was quickly the reply from Patton's aide.

"You better eat all those beans; you are going to need them. We got those Germans on the run," said Patton.

"Beans, no sir! We're serving up that great Bar B-Q you got us," said the cook standing in the mess tent right beside Pete.

"Bar B-Q? How the hell did these enlisted men get Bar B-Q? I sure as hell did not order Bar B-Q," thought Patton. He looked at his aide as if those two could read each other's minds and he, too, had no answer to where the delicious pork came from. Patton then turned to the group of guys at a nearest table.

"Hey boys, how's the chow?"

"It's great sir," rang out a chorus of hungry soldiers.

"Good, good, glad you boys liked it. Bar B-Q is one of my favorites and there's nothing too good for my men," said Patton as he made his way through the army of soldiers in the crowded mess tent, still working his way toward Sleepy and Pete's end of the table.

"How's the chow men?" he kept repeating as he patted the men on their backs and said his hellos. Then Patton's aide stopped the General and whispered something in his ear. Patton then looked down at Pete.

"Hey Smith, you're that boxer we have in our outfit. I heard you can put up a pretty good fight."

"Yes sir, I can at times, sir," Pete answered.

"You might be hearing from my aide, Pinkerton here, in the next few days. We're working on a boxing tournament throughout the armed forces. You'll get the information soon. Now you boys rest up and eat up. The war's waiting," Patton said.

"Yes sir," Pete and Sleepy answered. As the General again patted the two on their shoulders, he then turned to another table of soldiers and talked a little small talk to them as well. He then quickly worked his way around the tent and just like that he was gone.

Howard Isley, from Graham North Carolina, a kid from the same neck of the woods as Pete and Sleepy, looked as the General walked away from the tables. "He looks like a pretty good guy to me," said Howard.

"What the hell do you know Isley, you got here a couple of months ago right?" said Sleepy. "And besides, he didn't slap the shit out of you either," he said as he finished his second plate of Bar B-Q and got up from the table.

Pete added, "And by the way you have been here for over two months and that was the first time you saw the old man, right?"

"I see what you boys mean," Howard replied. "Oh hell, it's his war anyway; we just do the fighting and dying." With that they all got up from the table and left the mess tent.

"Anyone got a smoke?"

Chapter 7

The Cheater

THE CIGAR SMOKE in the tent was thick as London fog and the poker game had been going for what seemed to be all night and then some to Sleepy. There was one thing for sure in Sleepy's army every time the armored division seemed to stop or rest for a day or two a poker game would breakout. And that was just fine to him.

"I'll see that and raise you two bucks," said Sleepy, as he tried to speed things up and threw his two dollars down on the table.

"I call," was the answer from one of the soldiers sitting across from Sleepy.

"Two pair queens high," Sleepy replied, wearing a little smile on his face.

"That's pretty good, but not good enough," said the soldier sitting to the left of Sleepy.

" Damn lucky, you have been winning all night. Don't you think you need to give it a rest?" Sleepy suggested.

"Hey little man it's just my night. Ok?" said Mr. Lucky as he scooped up the money and raked it in with both hands. Hand after poker hand, this guy could not lose. A couple hours later, both the beer and the card game were getting flat for everyone else but Mr. Lucky. That was until the silence was broken by Bill and Speedy popping into the tent checking on their friend Sleepy. Everyone turned to the sound of the tent flapping when the door opened with a rush, as the two men came flying in the tent out of breath.

"What the hell are these two knot heads doing here?" someone in the game said.

"Sleepy we're here, let's go," said Bill Boyd, a tall, thin kid from Maryland with a starter kit mustache. He was always a real polite kid and Speedy's assistant drive in the tank.

"Hey there Sleepy, let's get going, times a wasting," said Speedy Kramer from Buffalo, New York. They called him Speedy because he was the number one driver of old Nellie Bell, their Sherman tank, but the funny thing was he did everything else so slow, but still a good old country boy Yankee with a lot of charm and with a love for gambling.

"Come on Sleepy, we got it," exclaimed Bill. "Let's go!" Both new comers seemed to be in a hurry.

"Go? I'm right in the middle of winning a bundle," Sleepy argued. Both boys looked down at the pile of money between the cigarette butts and beer cans.

"Bull, you ain't winning crap," said Mr. Lucky, who had been winning all night, as he put down his four aces. Everyone's jaw dropped wide open when the cards were shown.

"Four aces, shit," said Sleepy. "You see, I told you, ya'll boys are bad luck," as he quickly looked over at Bill and Speedy.

"Bad luck my ass! You're too dumb to know when to go," said Speedy.

And what Mr. Lucky did not know was that those two had been waiting for their cue from Sleepy for hours when they made their way in the tent. Speedy reached over and quickly pulled out the playing card that was hanging inside the sleeve of 'Mr. Lucky' with the four aces, and threw the bad hand of cards on the table that he had been hiding up his sleeve, and doing it all night.

"What the hell is this shit?" someone at the table said while grabbing Mr.Lucky's arm and exposing more cards.

"Hey friends I can explain," said Mr. Lucky, now the cheater.

"Friends my ass," said Sleepy as he grabbed some of the money off the table. "I'll just take my part."

About that time the rest of the men grabbed Lucky and started roughing him up a little, pushing him face first onto the table.

"Thanks, Sleepy," said Ransom, the big man dealing the cards. "I like to run a good clean game around here."

"You're welcome," said Sleepy. "Glad we could help. You boys take good care of Mr. Lucky, you hear."

With that said all three boys left the tent, as sounds of an ass whipping broke out in the poker tent. The three walked far away from both the poker game and the lights of camp. "Damn we are heroes," Bill said as they reached the tree line of camp.

"I knew that son of a bitch was a cheat!" said Sleepy.

"Hell yeah, Speedy called that one alright," Bill said.

Sleepy looked over to Bill with a question mark look on his face. "Speedy can't take all the credit; it was Pete that knew all about that deal. He worked for months with Ransom, the dealer, to set that up and it paid off pretty good I might say," said Sleepy, as he started counting his money.

"Pete? Where the hell is Pete anyway?" said Speedy as he looked around.

"Oh, he's still at the dance with some drunken girl," said Bill, stifling a laugh.

"No he's not. He's on patrol again.   But speaking of drunk… did you guys get it?" said Sleepy as he turned into lookout mode checking the area all around camp.

"We sure did," the two boys said as one of them pulled two mason jars out from behind the tree they were standing beside.

"Now that's what I call a reward!" said Sleepy as he took the first drink. "Damn! "

Chapter 8

Uncle Lou's Arrival

The warehouse was always a busy place with trucks and forklifts moving like a high school dance on Saturday night. Pete stood right in the middle of it with pencil and clipboard in hand checking off new inventory of the produce as forklifts and hand trucks moved all around him. "Hey Joe move those tomatoes to the front of the warehouse would ya," Pete ordered to the man on the fork lift.

"Will do boss man," he replied back at Pete. And on a dime the driver turned the machine in that direction.

As Pete was filling out the paperwork on the tomatoes he heard something. He thought he heard a bark, and as he turned around he saw an older man come walking up from behind with a little dog. "Sir we don't allow animals in here. No one but employees is allowed in this area sir," Pete shouted out to the stranger. As the stranger got closer Pete realized who he was and that he was no stranger at all.

"Hey that's ok, my nephew runs this place," in a real low scratchy voice, the old man said.

"Uncle Lou!" replied Pete. "What are you doing here?" They hugged as the dog danced at their feet.

"Just thought I would come by and see the next heavy weight champion of the world that just happens to be my nephew," said Lou as the little terrier kept up his dance.

"Is this the new Buster?" said Pete as he reached down and picked him up. "Hey little flea bag."

"Yea that's the newest one right there, not as feisty but real smart that one, he's a keeper," Lou said rubbing the little dog's head.

"Mom said you might be coming in town one of these days. Are you staying long?"

"We'll see," said Lou, hoping something good will happen this time in town. "We'll see," he repeated.

This was the Uncle of the world, and everyone in the family called him 'the wind' behind his back, because like the wind, he blew in and out of town and their lives all the time. And every trip back to home was one of feast or famine. He would show up in a new Packard sedan and a new wife, or on foot with everything he owned on his back. This trip was the latter, broken and on foot with his trusty companion. Lou was something else, part fight promoter and part flimflam man, a true character; he looked like a big dirty Santa Claus. He was a large man with a big barrel chest and his once white beard was yellowed from the cigar smoke. Tobacco stain drooled down the corners of his lips, and he still had a deep voice like a scratchy fog horn, but he was everything to Pete.

"Saw in the Charlotte paper where old Rock sent you a -flying across the ring a few weeks ago," said Lou.

"Yap, not the whole ring just most of it," Pete said, looking down at the floor, then he looked up at Lou and they both laughed.

Boxing was everything to Lou. Back in the day he was the North and

South Carolina Heavyweight champion, but failed to gain the Southern title after being defeated by Young Stribling in Atlanta in 1924. But he was a real good boxer, sparring with the likes of such noted fighters as Jack Sharkey, Primo Carnera, Jack Dempsey, Gene Tunney and Jim Braddock. He loved everything about the fight game, being a fighter, trainer, manager, or promoter. It did not matter to Lou, and he just loved every little part of the sport. He also knew he had a diamond in the rough with Pete, and knew his nephew was a scraper, with a thunderous uppercut, and had what it took to be a good fighter and a real contender someday. Lou wanted to see Pete make it in the sport he loved. So back home he came, broke poor and busted. But Lou knew back home would be the best place for him to be right now like so many times before. But this time was different with the war looming and all, plus for the first time in a long time Lou wanted to be here and wanted to be part of his family, and maybe settle down, for now, maybe.

"How many times you think old Rock Harden has been knocked out?" Lou asked Pete.

"I don't know, never I guess" said Pete.

Lou asked again about the last fight. "How many times you think he has gone the distance?"

"Fifteen rounds, never that I know of. He usually knocks them out in the first couple of rounds. I know he's forty four and zero and thirty seven of those are by knockouts. Did you know that?" said Pete.

"No, I didn't, but that's a pretty impressive record don't you agree?"

"And how many of those knockouts are yours…three. Let's see. Never gone the distance, and all wins are either knockouts or TKO's, in the first few rounds. Something to think about I would say," said old Lou rubbing his head in thought. "Something to train on as well," he added.

"Hey Chief, where you want these green beans," shouted the fork lift driver. And in an instant Pete had his mind back on work. He drew the chipboard like a revolver and quickly started back checking inventory.

He then looked back up at Lou and little Buster. "Sorry Lou, I've got to get back at it. You are staying for a day or two, right? " Lou knew he was holding up operations in the warehouse so he headed out the way he came.

"Sure thing Pete, I'll stay some. I'm going to see my sisters now. I'll see you at supper," Lou said.

"I'll see you there Lou, bye Buster," said Pete as he got back to work, walking over to the driver on the forklift.

Chapter 9

Waiting on Help

PETE'S BODY WAS KNOCKED OUT, but his mind was putting all the pieces together on what just happened.

"About dozen of us" he was thinking, were on the road on night patrol knowing that the Krauts were in the area. All of a sudden a flare, then gun fire broke out and we all ran for cover, and the closest thing was a cornfield. Pete was thinking, "Great choice dumb ass," knowing now it was all a setup to turn us toward the field full of land mines. Those smart S.O.B.s could not move us in this field any better than if they brought us here by trucks.

"I must have been out for hours," he thought," but how long? Maybe a good part of the night" he imagined. The sun was coming up now and the landscape looked like a horror movie. The fog covered the ground and bodies and body parts finished off the scene of carnage. Row after row of corn stalks and bodies, and in the middle of it all was Pete. One leg gone from just above the knee and Pete's other leg broken to bits, a bullet hole in his right arm and it too was broken, but he was still there.

"Are you ok?" a voice rang out.

Pete turned to looked up as best as he could to see, but there was nobody in his line of sight… Again the voice. "Stay right there. We will get you," the voice cried out again.

Pete was thinking he was dreaming but then he thought "Oh shit, No, don't!" Then he heard the blast. He quickly covered his face from the blast of dirt and mud. He was not dreaming. The person or persons who were coming to help just stepped on a mine themselves. "O' my God!" he thought. "Those poor sons of bitches just died for me." He would not believe it as he just stared into space, and a few more hours went by…

Pete was awoken by the sound of someone else calling out. This time they were on a bull horn saying "Don't move soldier. We're getting more help for you. Don't move!"

"NO shit," Pete was thinking. "You don't have to tell me twice." Time marched on as the sun's heat was on the rise as well, for what seemed like a couple of hours, and then Pete saw an outline of someone, no two bodies, in the distance. It was two Army medics with a stretcher, on their way to Pete. Then, without warning, machine gun fire broke the silence and once more a blast and more gun fire. And as fast as it started, once again it stopped, but this time for good.

"They, too, must have bought the farm," thought Pete. He was thinking of the two medics that just died trying to save him. The wait would start again as hours and hours slowly ticked by, which to Pete must have seemed like days as he lay there like bacon in the sun's heat and frozen in time.

"How could this be happening to me, and what the hell did I do to deserve this?" he thought. His brain was on fire with thought. "Please think of something else, anything, just get your mind right" Pete told himself. Girls, cars, news of the day, even baseball. That's it, baseball. "Just remember the games like on the radio" he thought. And that is exactly what he did. Pete started playing every game he could think of in his head just like he heard for years. The whole broadcast, not just the playing of the game but the whole thing. "We got to kill some time, right?"

"Today's starting lineup between the Detroit Tigers and your Chicago White Sox is brought to you by Lucky Strike cigarettes." This would kill hours as Pete lay there watching the game in his mind.

"There's Luke Appling standing patiently at second base watching, as Joe Kuhel the White Sox power hitter comes to bat here in the bottom of the seventh. Ballgame is tied three to three, here is the wind up and the pitch to Kuhel and he smashes it. Appling takes off from second and he is headed home. This ball is back, back, and gone as it sails over the centerfield wall for a two run homer and the crowd goes nuts here on the Southside at Comiskey Park". Don't forget sports fans the Yankees are coming. Be sure to get your tickets for this weekend's double header with the New York Yankee's and your Chicago White Sox, it's sure to be a great series as the pennant race is tightening up. You don't want to miss it."

Pete's mind would keep him entertained like this for hours, and fill the void with endless innings, not knowing if help would ever come, but it was one hell of a ball game.

Chapter 10

Bar-B-Q

THE WOODS WERE SILENT and so were the three drunken soldiers laying flat on their backs, with smiles on their faces. Those mason jars were filled of old home brew, sometimes called spring water, and better known as moonshine. Sleepy, Bill and Speedy were dead to the world in a drunken state as the woods came alive with sound.

"Sleepy, Speedy where are you guys?" called out Pete as he walked around the woods on the tree line knowing that's where the boys and he were to meet up. He had been out on patrol and could not get back in time for the card game. He then turned around to the sound of snores, and that's when he saw them all piled up around the same tree like cord wood. One still had the Mason jar balanced on his chest, as if he was still waiting for another drop of spring water.

"Get your ass up," Pete demanded as he started kicking at their feet. He was not in the mood to put up with a bunch of friends who have had a little too much of 'who hit John'. And coming off patrol and being the only one that wasn't drunk sucked as well.

"What is going on? O shit, what the hell!" they started shouting.

Pete just stood there with a smile on his face. "I guess you found the mason jars," he said.

"Damn Pete, you scared the shit out of us," said Sleepy as he jumped up spilling the moonshine all over himself.

"He ain't kidding," said Bill as he grabbed his pants and ran behind the closest tree to fix his situation.

"Did it work?" Pete asked.

"What? Oh, the card game?   Yes sir! " said Sleepy as he tried to straighten up and wipe off the shine running down his leg while trying to tuck in his shirt at the same time.

"Like a charm," claimed Speedy.

"I knew that guy was a cheat, replied Pete. "Just wish we could give back all the money that SOB took from everybody."

"I don't think you'll have to worry about that guy anymore. Those ol'boys were whipping his ass pretty bad when we left the tent.

"Yea, when that S.O.B. wakes up, his clothes will be out of style. He'll be out for awhile believe me Pete. Hell they didn't seem to mind when we helped ourselves to some of the money," explained Speedy.

"Money?" said Pete. "That wasn't in the plan."

"Plan, hell you were not even there," Bill shouted behind the tree.

"No, I wasn't. You're right Bill, I was on patrol guarding your butt," Pete explained as he started looking around at the woods like he heard something.

That was when they all realized they were not alone as they all heard a sound of movement and twigs breaking under foot. Someone was out there all right; the camp was abuzz with news about Germans being nearby all day. From combat training or just pure instant, they knew it. Pete kept talking as his eyes were fixed on the woods. Sleepy would be the slowest to pick up on it, but he too soon realized that Pete was stalling in his speech for a reason. And like a well oiled machine fixed on killing and knives on the ready all four men jumped at the predator at the same time. The silent woods came alive with all kinds of sounds at this point, as the gang found the enemy just like they thought, and there was no letting up.

"Hold that son of a bitch!" someone shouted, as knife cuts and fist blows found their mark.

"Don't let him go," cried another, grabbing and clawing with the sounds of screams and heavy breathing.

"I got him! Die you son of a bitch," said Sleepy as he buried his knife deep in his target.

"He ain't getting away now," another said.

As the cries and screams filled the air the camp awoke and the search lights started to pan to the surrounding area where the noise could be heard. The fight was in view now for the whole camp to witness the blood sport.

"O' shit, we killed him!" said Bill, as the body fell to the ground with a thug. They just stood there with the enemy's blood covering them from head to toe. There was blood everywhere, including all over the four hunters. Their eyes fixed on their subject as the spot lights lit up the once darkened woods. They stood there motionless as they came to the realization of what just happened.

"A pig, what... a damn pig," said Pete.

"What the hell?" said both Sleepy and Speedy as they too tried to catch their breath. A pig, that's right ... the boys in their drunken state had killed a wild boar....a hog, not a German soldier that had made his way into camp, but an Italian swine. The soldiers on duty ran down the see what was going on.

"I see you boys are on the ready at a minute's notice, "said the first Sergeant as he rushed to the scene of the crime."

" Sergeant we had no idea it was a pig," said Pete as he was getting himself back together and trying to wipe off some of the blood from the victim .

"I understand that," said the Sergeant as he quickly picked up on the situation from their bloodshot eyes to the smell of alcohol on their breath. "I believe you boys." Then, before the matter could be resolved the Sergeant turned as he looked up into the air. The sound of Germen war planes flew over head. The whistle of bombs being dropped from those planes caused the whole camp to react, and running for cover was now on everyone's mind.

"What about the hog?" Sleepy said to Pete as they ran for cover from the oncoming aerial attack.

"I got a plan," said Pete. "Just hurry up and don't 'Slaw' down," he laughed, as the whole gang ran for cover.

Chapter 11

Operation Husky

THE BEACH LOOKED LIKE A HUNDRED CAR train wreck stretching out for miles as hundreds of thousands of men and their machines filled the once empty beaches of the southwestern coastline of Sicily, near the town of Gela. This mechanized parade carried on as far as the eye could see, and the steam of men pouring in from the waves seemed endless.

The landing at Red Beach was not as tough as Pete expected, but he was reminded of danger every time he was drenched by the ocean spray of water that would hit him from all directions after each shell exploded by his troop carrier causing the water to pour in the landing craft. Reality crept in once again as the machine gun fire and mortar shells welcomed them as they disembarked from the landing craft. Hundreds of Allied soldiers, British, American and Canadians ran on the beach head after the battleships pounded the shoreline with a barrage of artillery shell during the sea to land battle that lasted roughly nine hours. The invasion of Sicily was on, aka "Operation Husky", which was a massive undertaking consisting of thousands of men and their supplies, which started in the early morning in the dark, and stayed constant throughout the day into the evening, with more and more every hour. The majority of tanks, trucks and supplies were being ferried to the beach from ships in LST's; Landing Ship, Tank ships. These ships could carry over 18 Sherman tanks and 160 troops directly onto the beach. The men called them L.S.T. which stood for long, slow, targets. But in fact out of the thousands that were produced only twenty or so were ever destroyed. Now the other vehicle used in the campaign was the DUKW, an amphibious vehicle, better known by the men affectionately as the DUCK, and was widely liked. This was the first time on this massive scale that the DUKW was used in combat and proved to be an important asset. In utilizing both types of vehicles, never before were men transported with such speed and accuracy.

This was Pete's first DUCK ride, half truck; half boat vehicle and fast, so fast most of the troops and crew on board got sea sick. By the time Pete and the boys made their way to old "Nellie Bell", the fighting was a mere skirmish. Only a couple of pill boxes were still in operation by the Germans and that too was short lived by the time the U.S. Rangers showed up with their flame throwers and the Army's "big red one's" First Division.

"How's she look Pete?" said Sleepy, as Pete made his way through his first inspection of their M4 Sherman tank which they had dubbed, Nellie Bell.

"Not too bad, she's full of gas, all one hundred and seventy five gallons worth, but she's got a few things we need to get squared away again. I need to get Howard to check on a couple of track shoes and that left front suspension wheel and have the boys to do a complete inventory on ammo and supplies. We don't know how long it's going to be before we get replenished. And be sure you check those fluid lines. We can't afford any saltwater getting in there."

This whole conversion was going on as machine gun fire was peppering the sand all around the men and tanks as they were loading up and preparing to leave their mustarded station.

"Will do Commander," said Sleepy as he crawled in the hatch and down the ladder.

"Hey Speedy, you and Bill climb back in and let's get her fired up." Speedy and Bill had stayed with the tank and drove Nellie on and off the LST.

"You got it Sergeant," said Speedy Kramer who was the driver, and Bill, his assistant driver. Both hopped in the two forward hutches in the front portion of the tank, and slid down into their assigned seats.

"Hey Pete," shouted Lt. Ray Brown. "We ain't got all day out here, get that thing buttoned up and let's get going Commander. We're burning daylight."

"Alright boys you heard the man, saddle up Ol'Nellie, we're rolling," said Pete, as he quickly climbed back on top of his Sherman making sure the fifty caliber was clean and ready. He then sat down inside the lid of the turret, getting his last look of the massive invasion of ships and landing craft before he closed the hatch and climbed down the ladder. He turned into the cramped and dark world and waited for his eyes to adjust to the dim light and took his seat.

"Ok, Speedy, put us back in the game," Pete said, as they started to drive off the beach head. The war was starting back up again, but this time the boys were in Sicily. The landing had taken a lot longer than the headquarters had anticipated, days instead of hours. German air cover was giving them a fit, and the waters just in front of the beach head were full of sandbars. This too caused anguish to the planners. But once the Rangers seized possession of the airfield here at Gela, and the ships 'guns kept up their pounding of the enemy's position on the beach, things were looking up for the Allied forces, and the tanks could finally start rolling on to the landscape of Sicily.

Explosions rattled the tanks and its occupants, as the tanks' track shoes dug deep into the blood soaked sand of Sicily. Pete and the boys were at the ready, eyes wide open and hearts pounding as the tanks lined in single file and worked their way off the beachhead. Dozens of infantry soldiers fell in behind the Shermans as they worked their way off the beach onto the dirt road headed to Gela and Ponte Olivo, without knowing what was around the next turn.

"Bill over to your right, over there," Pete called out into Bill's headset. Without hesitation Bill grabbed the handle to his thirty caliber Browning and did quick work of the two Germans with grenades in their hands.

"Ok boys, stay alert. Good job Bill," said Pete as he looked down and back at Nellie, checking on Sleepy and making sure he was on the ready with the seventy-six millimeter shells for the big gun.

"You good Sleepy, is everybody good?"

"We're all good here boss," said Sleepy, giving Pete the thumbs up, and "all good" ring throughout the turret.

"O'right men, lets spread out a little bit as we get over the hill and don't forget to check your six. We don't want anybody sneaking up on us from the rear," said LT. Brown

"Roger that," echoed down the regiment of tanks as they slowly crept over a small ridge down in a ravine. And then there was an order of all stop. Up and down the line all tanks hit the brakes.

Looking out through his periscope Pete was eyeballing about twelve tanks, half of which were Renault thirty- fives that were French made tanks. They had been captured by the Germans and sold to the Italians; a lightweight tank not known for their speed or anything else but still a pretty good tank. The other tanks in play were Fiat 3000's. Now these looked more like something you would see in World War I. The Fiat was Italian made, but made in the thirties, a two man machine with a very small gun tank and a top speed of thirteen miles per hour.

Pete liked his odds, but before he could lick his chops he heard a familiar rumble and at that point his smile was completely erased. Coming over the horizon were a platoon of German tigers. Now there's a tank! Heavy armor, V-12 engine and the first tank to have mounted an 88 millimeter cannon and in the right conditions it could outrun, outshoot and maneuver about any Sherman. But there were two weaknesses with the Tiger and they were the rear end was an easy target because of a slow moving turret, and the tank tracks were suspect to break down a lot so they couldn't turn as quickly as they would like in fear of losing a track. Other than that she was as tough as they came in the world of tanks. And Pete was staring straight at four of them as they advanced from the grove of olive trees like the prowling tiger which they were named after.

"Blue dog to Red Leader, Blue dog to Red Leader, we have four Tigers to our north, northwest, needing assistance, over," said Lt. Brown, while everyone held their breath. Brown gave out the coordinates.

Pete, looking out the periscope, noticed two plumes of smoke coming from the barrels of the tanks in the distance. A few seconds later came a couple of explosions that hit just short of their target but directly in front of Pete and the gang, as a few R-35's tested their big gun's range. No one moved. All the Shermans sat waiting as ordered.

"Roger that," said Lt. Brown as he received word from headquarters. "Hold tight boys, help is on its way," said Brown in his headset. And he was right, for in less than a minute the men could hear that familiar whistle sound of rocket noise and heard it getting louder as the shells from the big guns of the U.S.S. Boise and her sister ship the U.S.S. Savannah, demonstrated their effectiveness as the bombs rained down on the Tigers. The whole pack of Axis tanks started to disperse and run for their lives. They had no chance, they were sitting ducks as three out of the four Tigers were completely destroyed. One was left, but with a change of mind it quickly headed in retreat.

"Alright boys let's do some damage, head'em out," shouted Lt. Brown as his group of Shermans gunned their Detroit motors and started to pull out of the ravine. In quick order the Shermans were in charge of the situation, picking off the out gunned R-thirty-fives and Fiat three thousands like fishing in a barrel. The American infantry had waited down the hill till the coast was clear and then they too made their advancement on the enemy

"Speedy hit it hard to the right, enemy on the left flank!" shouted Pete, as he called out directions to Kramer. "Sleepy fire," as the speeding shell hit the tank track off the fleeting R-35. "Hit'em again," Pete ordered to the crew of the Nellie Bell as they responded to a second shot from their big gun causing the enemy's tank to explode into flames.

The sky was dotted with planes as the air was now full of noise. Bombs and machine gun fire came raining down from the sky as the Allies air force fought its way to be superior over their German counterparts, as they fought and took over the air space in the entire region. The enemy's infantry fled into the grove of olive trees hoping for cover, but were quickly picked off by the dive bombing P-38 Lightings and the powerful machine gun fire of the pursuing P-51 Mustangs, spraying the rest of the scattered few as the war planes made sure of victory as they mopped up the land, air and sea campaign making Operation Husky a rout as it moved inland.

"Thank God for the sea and air support," thought Pete as he opened the hutch to Nellie and told the rest of the boys to stand down. The crew took a sigh of relief, knowing it could have been a lot worse. Pete observed the battlefield as his comrades- in- arms one by one destroyed the enemy's tanks, and as far as Pete was concerned this battle was all but over, for now anyway. But the fight for Sicily would take months, not days and thousands of souls would be lost, ensuring that Hitler was stopped for good.

Chapter 12

Homecoming

"SO LET ME GET THIS STRAIGHT. You believe Pete has what it takes to be the heavy weight champion of the world, right?" said Knobby in the kitchen as she washed the purple hull peas in the sink before she was going to shell them. Knobby was Lou's oldest sister, a real nice lady, but a lot like Lou. She was hardheaded to a point, to where she would push back as hard as you pushed her and maybe a little harder. It seemed to run in the family.

Lou was sitting in the living room at the piano, his favorite place, as the two talked between rooms about Pete's future, and Lou kept playing the ivories to "She'll Be Coming Around the Mountain".

"That's right; well to a point I guess, or at least maybe not the champ, but a real good contender" Lou argued with his older sister. There's good money in it Knobby. That boy could go places."

"A contender, go places, what, like you?" said Knobby as she turned to see who was coming in the back door. The back screen door opened and in came Aileen, Lou and Knobby's youngest sister. Aileen was a tom boy and the youngest of the seventeen children. Lou and Knobby were a lot older than she. Aileen was only a couple of years older than Pete. She came to live with her sister Knobby and her husband Jim, when their parents died a few years back.

"Lou, you are a sight for sore eyes," Aileen said as she ran into his big bear arms and gave him a big hug.

"Hey sugar bugger, how's my favorite baby sister doing?"

"Just great Lou. Check out the size of the fish I got. It'll be good eating. Play some more Lou. I heard you playing that old piano all the way down to the pond. That's how I knew it was you".

"Sure, sure, but first tell me why a girl as pretty as you is fishing, and fishing alone. You should be dating, going dancing and those kinds of things."

"It's my fault," said Knobby. "I let her hang out with Pete and his crew all the time. She is just like'em."

"You don't let me do nothing. I do what I want to do, big sister," said Aileen with a smile on.

Lou turned and looked at Aileen. "I guess you like to prize fight as well," he said as he laughed.

" No Lou, but I can sell the heck out of those fight tickets, and between rounds I sell peanuts and popcorn. It's fun!" Aileen was excited just thinking about it. "Now play that thing," she said looking once again at the piano.

"She's just like Daddy," Lou thought, "and gets excited over life itself and hardheaded as hell, but fun to be around." She was always his favorite. He turned to get started playing the piano again.

"I could hear you two talking about Pete's fighting all the way down to the pond. I think he is going to be a great fighter but the good Lord has bigger plans for that man. He has too much on the ball to be just a fighter, no offense Lou," said Aileen, still holding the fish while she talked.

Lou stopped and turned away from playing the piano again. "None taken, but what do you mean by 'on the ball?"

"Are you kidding?" Aileen's defense went up. "He has leadership. His friends follow him like a dog; and Pete has more charisma than all his buddies put together. He has what they call, the It Factor. You both know that." Aileen stopped preaching and watched Lou and Knobby look at each other and agree.

"Baby sister is right," Lou added. "No one knows what life has in store for any of us." And no one knew that better than Lou. Life is a question at best. But if anyone could stand out as being special in this town it was Pete and they all knew it.

"Heavyweight championship my eye," said Knobby, as she got the fish from Aileen and placed them in a bowel to clean till she could clean out the sink of peas, and cook the fish for dinner. "You two are crazy. That boy is too smart to volunteer to get his brains kicked in for money."

Aileen looked at Lou. "Well if you're not going to play that thing I'm going to my room and get cleaned up. Willie is coming over and we are going out tonight dancing." Lou just sat there with a smile on his face at that piece of information. "See Lou, most people are more than what they look or act like," said Aileen, as she turned and went down the hall to get ready. "Oh by the way, welcome home Lou," she shouted.

Lou just shook his head, as to say "that girl is something," as he started once again to play the piano, but this time loud enough for all to hear, knowing he was welcomed home.

Chapter13

It's About Time

EVERY DAY THAT PASSED IN THE MINEFIELD was worse than the other. Freezing at night and burning up hot all day, minutes and hours seemed to slow down even more. The slowness of each minute passing was as painful as his wounds and Pete was stuck there in that field just waiting for somebody to find him, or to die.

"Please God, either save me or bring me home," he prayed. "I would rather die than have someone die trying to save me again, and how many have died trying to do just that," thought Pete.

He would fade in and out, becoming weaker as the minutes and hours seemed to crawl by at a snail's pace. Pete knew his time on this earth was about up and there was nothing he could do. He lay there watching as buzzards circled over head and the summer day steam bath started warming up again. He had tried to use his poncho as a tent to block out the sun's rays but it was hard to do with one hand and a broken arm. But some cover was better than nothing and it worked to a point, and he used the mud as sun tan lotion as well. He had his pistol, and bayonet blade layed out in the open so if he needed quick use of either they were handy. He had not eaten in days and the sight of the corn stalks made him that much hungrier. Too bad it was too early in the season for corn and there were no ears on the stalks. Besides he would probably blow himself up crawling to get some nourishment.

"Just my luck," he thought. "I'm entering day three, and it's going to be hot as hell again today. O' God, how much more can I take?" he said to himself as he checked the amount of water that was left in his canteen. It sounded like a couple of swallows as he shook and twirled the metal container to hear the water in the bottle, and knowing he had to conserve and ration himself, he then placed it too, out in front of his other possessions like the pistol and knife.

Even the hot and steamy weather was against him. He tired of trying to keep his mind off of the situation, but once again he put his mind back to being a kid of ten or eleven, enjoying the good times back home. This time doing kid stuff like running down the dirt path behind his house into the magical world of the woods, where he could escape from reality and be transformed into Dick Tracy or Robin Hood, even Blackbeard the pirate. Deep in the forest Pete could be anyone his heart desired. Today he would play Captain Hook, as he walked along the narrow path down to the creek to set sail his balsawood fleet of wooden boats. Starting the adventure Pete would put in at the uncharted waters up steam from the water falls at old slippery rock, which was lined and covered with slick green algae and moss, a good foot and a half drop off. But the rock everyone really loved which lay beside of that one was the picnic rock, a huge slab of granite where Pete's family would come to cool off and sit and hang their feet in the cool waters. Of course they would have picnics on the massive slab throughout the hot summer weekends. Then, after the flotilla had survived the falls at slippery rock, they maneuvered around the rocks and jetties of the creek and found themselves under fire by a volley of incoming artillery of bombing dirt clogs and rocks. The few who survived were welcomed at the finish line by Pete as he picked up the damaged vessels at the old sandy hole, a large sandbar about fifty yards downstream from where the journey had begun. Hours would be spent in the woods and all the while you would be sheltered from the hot summer heat under the canopy of trees. But most of the time in the dog days of summer Pete would want to go fishing and swimming, and there was no where better than at his favorite watering hole, John Long's pond. The pond looked like a lake to Pete and boys. But on a hot summer day like this one, that's when he would head out on his bike and meet Sleepy and rest of the gang and swim for hours and just do boy stuff; horse play and mess around with each other till someone got mad, build a tree house out in the woods and of course learn how to smoke a cigarette. Growing up in Hopedale, North Carolina was a great place for a kid. But then the pain caused Pete's thoughts to switch back to now, as reality crept back into his mind to the present. Hour after hour and still no relief, hardly any water, no food for days and wounds starting to bleed out even more, and still the heat. He thought again of the woods and the canopy of trees.

Pete's daydreams were suddenly stopped by the sound of more gun fire as it broke the silence once again. Pete could hear the sound of trucks and men, and gun fire, but this time there seemed to be no return fire. It was all coming from the same direction. Like a mirage or some kind of bizarre realization, he could not understand if the things that were happening were real or not. Pete was feeling like he was punch drunk after spending so much time in that broken cornfield. It was like being pounded in the ring for days and days of a non-stop beating. He turned his head toward the sounds of a group of soldiers that were right in front of him who were making their way slowly through the mine field. They appeared to be in slow motion, probing the plowed field inch by inch with their bayonets, carefully overturning each stone, making sure not to detonate a mine buried under the soil beneath their feet. All the while Pete watched as if they were coming to someone else's aid, and not his. It was as if he was watching an old Van

Johnson or Errol Flynn movie as the soldiers worked hard at their task, inching their way a little closer. It was like watching a movie in a theater; all Pete needed was a bag of popcorn, a Baby Ruth candy bar and an ice cold Cheer-wine soda. The whole episode had to be playing tricks on his mind. He had not seen anyone in days and now the 7th Army appeared to be arriving.

"Hey, over here soldier, can you hear me?" a Medic asked as he pick-up the pace of his approach, moving the dirt with his bayonet as quickly as he could. Pete's blurry eyed stare gave the impression of a zombie as he watched more of the so called war movie.

Pete broke out of his trance as his weak voice spoke out very faintly, "Yes."

"Hey everybody, over here!" someone cried out, as he too found Pete in the cornfield.

" Here he is," another called. "Get the medic." It was if Patton himself had ordered the army of men to the rescue and the heavens had opened up. Pete could not believe his eyes. He was not dreaming and it was not a mirage, as he cleared his eyes to see himself surrounded by the U.S. Army. Tears flowed down his face. Pete could not believe it, after all this time.

One of the medics grabbed Pete by the arm. "We got you buddy, just hang in there," as he and others started working on their patient. Administering drugs and I.V. , they very carefully removed some of his gear, and bandaged some wounds as they got him ready to transport him out of hell.

And just like that, this part of his anguish was over.

"I have been saved, thank you God," Pete thought. He smiled and grabbed some mud and dirt with his good hand as he was being slowly placed on the stretcher. He would not remember any more of the rescue as his eyes closed and once again his world went black, but this time he was safe.

Chapter 14

Training Day

"NO, NO, NO, YOU DON'T WAIT for the fighter to come to you, you go to him," shouted Lou. Pete stood there doing his best impression of a stone statue as his sparring partner kept hitting him with left jabs and a strong right punch over and over as Pete took the beating. "Stop, I've seen enough of this stuff. Damn it Pete, you ain't the punching bag here, you have got to move those feet. Go after him boy, don't wait for him. You be the aggressor. Lou climbed under the ropes and walked over to Pete shaking his head.

"Yap, I did that before," said Pete feeling sorry for himself as he thought once again of his loss in the Hard Rock fight.

Lou looked at Pete, knowing he was thinking of the Hard Rock fight and said, "Well this time you'll be boxing, not brawling and with your head on straight and eyes open, plus I'll be in your corner this time."

"I know Lou," said Pete shaking head as to agree with Lou.

As they stood in the ring at the old broken down Broad Street gym, Lou looked over at Tig Brown, Pete's sparring partner. "Have a sit Tig, I need to talk to my boy," Lou instructed the sparring partner standing in his corner waiting for more orders.

"Sure thing boss," he said, breathing pretty hard as he took off his head gear and wiped off the sweat with a towel. "Sure thing boss," said Tig, as he took a seat on the corner stool to catch his breath.

"Now listen to me Pete. You two are just flitting around out there. Now look son, everyone has a fighter that gets in their head, but there are more guys to fight than Hard Rock Harden and a lot of those folks are better than him. So first we got to get you to quit beating yourself up and work on fighting someone else", Lou said.

"I Know Lou and I'm trying to, but I can't beat him."

"Shut up, again we ain't fighting him. Now come here. We are going to try something different." Lou pulled out a piece of string and tied Pete's right hand back behind him. "Now, this time you are going to punch with just your left hand. Try that," he said. "And we are going to do this 'till your power punch comes from your left side. I'm going to make you a new boxer, one that will be hard to train against." Pete shook his head in agreement.

"OK Tig get your butt up, we got training to do," shouted Lou.

So for weeks Pete fought left-handed, so much he even ate with his left hand. But getting the muscles to do something different is one thing. Making it second nature in your mind is another thing all together. Day in and day out, for months the two men worked on it for hours every day. Pete never worked so hard in his life. He quit taking the bus to work and every day he ran to and from. He would wake up around five am and run from Hopedale, which was out in the country, to town, about five miles each way, everyday. He would spend hours in the gym working on the speed bag that would build endurance and timing of his punches. From thousands of sit-ups to jumping rope and hours after hours pounding the heavy bag, to working on his breathing and building his stamina to go the full fifteen rounds Pete was now the total package. And after weeks and countless hours of training Lou turned to Pete as they were waiting in the locker room and said, "Son you got it. You are as ready as you will ever be."

"Sounds good to me," said Pete. And the two just smiled at each other as they walked out of the locker room into the packed arena to the cheers of hundreds of boxing fans.

Chapter 15

Girl of his Dreams

MILDRED WILKES WAS A REGISTERED NURSE FROM OHIO, but all her friends called her Millie. And like the posters said, "YOU ARE NEEDED NOW," so she quickly volunteered to join the Army Nurse Corps after her oldest brother Ben was killed at Pearl Harbor. Millie was a strong minded girl but for some reason she seemed to be a little afraid to go down the steps by herself as she stood in the entrance of the USO club overlooking the crowd from the top of the stairs. The room was full of laughter, noise and smoke that circled up to the ceiling as the band played the hit song "In the Mood." She was a tall girl, about five feet ten inches, wide in the shoulders, with a small waist and a face like an angel, a real beauty. She hoped that her beauty would hide the fact that she stuttered. Not much, but her speech impediment was something she worked very hard on. She had waited for what seemed like an hour for her girl friends Lisa and Betty, but since those two turned out to be a no show, she decided to go join the fun in the crowd below on her own. And just like in the movies the band and the crowd seemed to focus on her as she made her way down the stairway.

She was truly a beauty and it seemed as though she captured everyone's attention. The crowd watched her gracefully make her way into the room. But there is where the story book, movie scene ends. Just as she stepped down onto the last step Pete Smith seemed to come out of nowhere, as he came barreling in from the side door with drinks in both hands and nothing else on his mind but to stay balanced and not spill the handful of drinks. He heard the shouts of "watch out, lookout, stop!" but his body just could not react in time as he ran right over Millie and down they both went.

"Oh, you, you, you, fool!" she cried.

Like a car wreck, the two landed in a heap at the bottom of the landing. Drinks and glasses were everywhere and their two bodies lay out on the floor while the whole place held their breath. It was like a movie after all, starring the Max Brothers! Her hair and dress were wet with drink and her makeup was melting down her face. Pete was still wondering what had just happened and was trying to catch his breath at the same time. "I'm sorry, oh gosh, I'm so sorry," said Pete, as he was trying to straighten her hair and dress.

"Get, get, get, your hands off of me you, you big ape!" shouted Millie. "Don't touch me, me , me you fool!"

Pete stopped and looked her straight in the eyes, as if nothing had happened and they had just met. "Hey, my name's Pete, Sergeant Pete Smith," he said, in a calm voice while he was still on the floor looking up at the girl of his dreams. And with that the band members and the whole crowd of people started laughing and applauding. The whole scene was pure mayhem. Millie could not believe what just happened. She had no choice but to stand up, clean herself off and stick out her hand to help Pete up.

"Well solider, you, you, sure know how to knock a lady off her feet!" The crowd was now cheering for the couple as Pete made his way to his feet. The two just looked at each other for several seconds as the magic of the moment sunk in. Pete could not believe what he was looking at. She was beautiful.

"Can I have this dance?" Pete asked, as the band started on cue.

"I hope you can, can dance better than you can walk soldier," she said with a laugh and the two danced to String of Pearls.

"Again I'm sorry. I guess I've had a little too much to drink ," said Pete. "We're moving out again tomorrow and getting drunk seemed to be the thing to do. Gosh you're pretty.   What's your name again?"

"It's Millie, I mean Mildred, Mildred Wilkes," she said as she looked away in search of her girl friends.

"Millie, that's a pretty name," Pete said, with stars in his eyes.

"No never mind," she thought. "He is still drunk, but big and darn good looking to boot," she thought.

"Look, I'm going out on patrol tomorrow night, but I'll be back in a few days. Can I call you? I promise Millie, I am a good guy and I would love to see you again."

"You don't know me, we, we, just, just, met, or wrecked. Anyway I, I, I, don't know you."

"I know you don't. That's why people date, so they can get to know each other better silly."

She turned her head and smiled. She was impressed by his dancing. Not bad at all she thought, as the dance was coming to an end. "OK, sure, we'll go out next time you're in town. That, that, will be fine."

"Really, you will? That's great," said Pete with a smile on his face you could not wash off.

"Now I'm sorry, but I do have to go and find my friends. I'll see, see, you in a few days." Millie turned away from Pete with that same smile that would not quit and walked out of the USO club.

Pete stood on the dance floor for the longest time. The next song had started, and he was still thinking, "what a girl, I must be dreaming."

Chapter 16

The Ticket

"YOU GOING TO GIVE ME A TICKET OR NOT," shouted Pete, sitting in his Hudson with both his temper, and engine racing. He pulled his hat down over his eyes and started mumbling under his breath while drumming his fingers on the steering wheel. The policeman took his time as he slowly approached the vehicle while he adjusted his hat and gun belt.

"Hey Pete, that wasn't me driving like a mad man down through Bullet Road over a hundred miles an hour," said Pete's cousin Dud. Dud was a big, stocky, barrel-chested man with thick gray wiry hair and was always a little jealous of Pete when they were growing up, if the truth was known.

Pete jumped up in the seat. "Well cousin, oh excuse me, Mister Policeman, I guess that's why they call it Bullet Road," Pete said in a defiant tone.

"Well, I can tell you this mister smarty pants, they don't call it drunkard's lane," said Dud, as he reached in the car and pulled out a bottle of Old Crow whiskey that was sitting in plain view behind the driver's seat. Pete was surprised at what he saw. He had no idea it was there. "Well, well, looky here, looks like the champ's going to the lock up tonight," Dud said with a grin on his face.

"Oh come on Dud. You know you put that there last night when we were double dating, and since when does the police chief sit out on Bullet Road and hand out speeding tickets?"

"Yea, who you think the judge is going to believe, you or me? Now get out of the car." Dud grasped Pete by the arm and tried to help him out.

"Get you damn hands off me!" Pete yelled as he fought to get his one leg out of the car.

"Wait a minute," Dud said, as he started thinking about the situation, knowing he did put the whiskey in the car and not wanting to get caught. "Just stop. Stay in the car Pete. Stop, I don't want to put you in jail. I just want you to get your head straight boy." Pete stopped and started to get back in the car. "We all understand what you must be going through but you can't keep this up. You are going to kill your damn self or somebody else." Dud tried to help get Pete back inside the car, but Pete pulled himself back in and shut the door.

"Are you going to give me a ticket or not?" Pete shouted.

"Damn you're hardheaded! You haven't heard a word I said."

"I'll tell you what," said Pete. "The day some son of a bitch blows your leg off we can talk, till then get the hell out of my face officer."

Dud shook his head. "We all care about you Pete. Aunt Knobby sent me out here to talk some sense in you. You need help and you need to go see Dr. Manus, or Preacher Mack. You have got to talk to someone. Can't you see it's eating you up? You are not the same person you used to be Pete and we all miss that guy," Dud said as he handed Pete the speeding ticket.

"I didn't know you cared so much." Pete waved the speeding ticket in Dud's face. "What's this, a ticket of love? Thanks a lot cousin. Why don't you give this here ticket to the old Pete you've been talking about," Pete said as he quickly grabbed the ticket out of Dud's hand and put the car in gear. "What you all need to understand is I'm trying." With that Pete squalled the tires as he took off from the side of the road leaving Dud standing in a cloud of dust.

"That boy is messed up," Dud said as he stood there watching Pete drive off like a mad man.

As Pete raced off he started wrestling with the steering wheel with one hand and searching under the driver's seat with the other. "There you are," he said out loud as he pulled the half empty bottle of whiskey out from underneath. "That's what I'm talking about. What the hell does he know?" Pete said as he put the bottle to his lips and took a big drink. Thinking of Dud's words "we all understand what you are going through," Pete gave a laugh and threw the ticket out the window of the speeding car in little pieces.

Chapter 17

Pain and Confusion

A SMALL DIRT CLOD LAY in a box on top of the night stand beside the bed in the dark, long room of the amputee ward of the hospital. The hospital was like a battlefield itself, row after row of beds full of pain, confusion and fear. Pete lay there day after day with a blank look on his face, wondering what was next on this bizarre journey. From the field hospital in Italy to this one, the Royal Sussex Hospital in Brighton, England, it had been a whirl wind tour for sure.

Pete had one leg badly broken in several places, two bullet wounds and a broken right arm and, worst of all, was the loss of most of his left leg. The doctors told Pete about the possibility of destruction of his blood supply, which meant the loss of the main artery and collateral arteries, so the amputation was a must. The leg was missing from just north of the knee, called a transfemoral amputation. Pete was also suffering from the cuts and bruises all over his body. In short, he was a mess in both body and spirit. Battered and broken, Pete knew he would never see the ring again or be anything like he was before.

And by the looks of what he was seeing in the hospital there was a great chance he was not getting out there alive. Pain was everywhere and not in short supply... men moaning and screaming all day and night and more coming in daily. It was an endless sea of broken men and tired nurses. For days Pete seemed to do nothing but stare into the darkness.

"You going to drink your orange juice?" said the patient in the bed beside Pete. Pete was still in a state of confusion when he answered the man.

"What orange juice? No, I don't know, oh hell you can have the drink. I ain't going to drink it, I don't want it," said Pete as he lay looking away from the sound of the man's voice, twisting in his bed.

"Hey what part of New York are you from?" joked the soldier, looking over to catch Pete's reaction.

"I'm not from New York," said Pete.

"No shit! That was a joke Hillbilly. My name's Frankie. I'm from New York….up state, Buffalo area. "

"Oh yea I'm sorry," said Pete, still not looking at who was talking

"That's ok Hillbilly. You don't have to say a thing. It's pretty hard on everyone the first couple of months."

"Months!" shouted Pete. "Months? I ain't going to be here that long am I?" Pete asked.

"Calm down soldier. I'm sorry, you're right. It won't be that long," Frankie said to calm Pete down. "You will be out of here in no time."

"God I hope so," Pete sighed. "I'm ready to get home."

"Where's that?" Frankie asked.

"The Tar Heel state, North Carolina," Pete said with pride. About that time a patient cried out for a nurse, and then another called for one. It was like a pack of dogs. One starts barking and then the whole bunch chimes in. That's the way the noise of the room would start up every time. Pete and Frankie decided not to fight it and just sat back in their beds and listened to the sounds of pain and confusion once again.

A few minutes passed and by the time the noise calmed downed Frankie once again spoke. " 'Bout that orange juice," said Frankie.

Pete, still not looking at him shouted, "I said you can have it! Just get it yourself. O hell, here, I'll get it." Pete turned over in the bed and got the glass of juice from the night stand, but then he froze. Without thinking he dropped and broke the glass of juice on the floor and stopped talking. He looked at Frankie as the realization of where he was sunk in and realized the new friend he was talking to was an amputee as well, with no arms or legs. Pete had no words to say. He just starred for the longest time.

Frankie broke the ice. "At least now you know you're not going through this alone Hillbilly." Pete started to give the whole ward a look-over and that's when he finally noticed that everyone there was missing something. There was not one whole person in the place. He was in shock as his eyes roamed over the sight of all the amputees...missing arms, legs, feet, hands, and worse, like Frankie, were the ones missing all the above.

"It's like watching the train station scene in Gone with the Wind when Atlanta was burning ain't it?" said Frankie.

"I don't know." said Pete. "I didn't see it. I was drafted before that one got to the movie house in my neck of the woods. I sure am glad I didn't. This is horrible." He quickly turned his head away once again in the bed and closed his eyes.

"You're right, it's bad alright, but trust me you're one of the lucky ones. It can always be worse," Frankie said as he looked over at a fellow patient that had just passed away with the bed sheets pulled up over his face.

The two did not say anything else for the rest of the day.

Pete stayed withdrawn in his bed and huddled under the covers like a child scared to venture beyond the security of his blanket day after day. Pete could not make himself watch as the hospital ward well exceeded its maximum capacity with the steady stream of more and more broken and wounded soldiers as they arrived daily. He still could not believe his circumstances of being an amputee. How, why, what did I do to desire this, a litany of self-pity and why not, he certainly deserved it. But he truly was not the only one. Thousands of men were brought to Royal Sussex which was built in 1828 and it was overwhelming to everyone involved. And to ease the pain of overcrowding a lot of the over flow patients were sent to the newer St. Richard's Hospital which was built in 1938 and located in Chichester, in West Sussex England. But not Pete, he was to endure long enough till he would be shipped stateside after a four month stay, hiding safely under the security of his blankets. As for Frankie, he didn't make it home, and neither did thousands of men. Frankie was right after all. Pete was lucky and hopefully someday he would know it too.

Chapter 18

Bad Timing

"THAT'S SOME STUFF about Pete ain't it," said Bill, as he and Speedy were laying under the R-975 Whirlwind engine in the back of Nellie Bell, their M4 Sherman tank. With the sun at its highest they truly wished she had broken down under a shade tree, not out in the full sun at the hottest time of day. There wasn't a tree to be seen for miles, and they were stuck, broke down on the side of the road in the middle of nowhere and were tired of waiting for the repair truck to show up.

"Hand me that crescent wrench Bill," said Speedy as he tried to stop the oil leak of the nine cylinder air-cooled radial motor as fast as possible using his finger to plug the hole. The two were covered in the stuff, but they just kept talking and working on the big Continental Motors engine as the oil flowed out. "Quick Bill, we're going to drown in the stuff, hurry." Bill handed Sleepy the wrench and he went fast to work as the oil flow slowed down to a dribble and then it finally stopped. They both lay back with a sigh of relief and relaxed under Nellie Bell. At least they were in the shade.

"Well, thank goodness he's alive," said Speedy, returning to the conversation about Pete. As they talked an approaching dust trail from a speeding vehicle appeared out of nowhere in the distance and was quickly headed their way up the winding dirt road.

"We lost a lot of good men that night, Speedy.   I still can't believe Howard died. He wasn't with us two months."

"Two months, that's a lot longer than a lot of good men get around here with old blood and guts on the gas paddle, twenty four hours a day, and seven days a week. Oh damn it!" he shouted as the wrench slipped off the nut. "This tank was a piece of shit when it was brand new," said Speedy as he hit his hand on the radial aircraft engine for the hundredth time.

They both turned quickly towards the sound of a speeding jeep slamming on the brakes as it pulled up close to the back of Nellie. They both jumped, hitting their heads once again on the engines old pan. "Hey fella, watch out! We're under here, dumb ass!" said Bill. The driver looked a little wild eyed as he started to get out of his jeep. "It's just our luck to go through this whole war and get killed by a damn jeep!" muttered Bill.

"Sorry men, I didn't see you two under there," said the tall and lanky driver as he bent down and saw the two under the tank. I'm so sorry. Anyway, can you fellows tell me where can I find a Sergeant Pete Smith? I got a letter here for him from head quarters," said the private, trying to help Bill and Speedy up from under the tank, and waving the letter around like a white flag of surrender.

Bill started to talk. "Well he's not here. You see, he was..." Speedy cut Bill off.

"That's right," said Speedy as he stopped Bill from talking. "You see he had to go see the Lieutenant about something. What you got there? I'll make sure he gets it." Speedy reached out and tried to grab the letter. Both men had a good hold of it as they played tug of war over the letter.

"Wait," said the soldier. "Wait, don't tear the thing," and with that,

Speedy let go and the soldier pulled it back into his possession. "Wait pal, I can't give it to you. I have my orders. Besides, you're not him," as he looked and saw the name Kramer embroidered on his uniform.

"Look here private," said Speedy as he grabbed the letter once more. "I'm a corporal. That means I outrank you. Besides, Pete's our buddy and you can trust us," said Speedy with a sheepish grin, as his pencil thin mustache curled up on one side of his mouth, and he could feel the private loosening his grab.

"I don't know fellows. I could get in a lot of trouble."

"Here," said Speedy as he handed him two packs Lucky Strike cigarettes, then three. With that the Private let go of the letter and gladly let Speedy have it.

"OK, there you go then," he said, as he quickly jumped back in the jeep and started to pull off. "Now make sure he gets it guys. It's important, it could be his ticket out," he said as he pulled off in the jeep.

"Will do," said Bill, cleaning himself off, anticipating Sleepy opening the letter.

"You can bet on it," said Speedy, as the two of them tore into the letter addressed to Pete.

From: Head quarters 7th Army

General Patton's offices

Dear Sergeant Smith,

You have been selected to represent the 7Th Army stateside, in New York City, August 4th at Madison Square Garden to help support war efforts in the U.S. bond drive. You will be participating In the War Bond Fight Contest in Madison Square Garden Arena along with: Sergeants Joe Louis, Billy Conn, Private Bob Montgomery, Private Sidney 'Beau-Jack' Walker. Your travel orders will be sent to you ASAP

as soon as we get further approval from the offices of the Allied Commander. I know you will conduct yourself honorably at all times and represent the 7th Army with pride and humility. I extend my appreciation and well wishes upon you. With your help and all the other participants' contributions we should sell a tremendous amount of war bonds which will help us defeat the enemy. -

Good luck and God speed,

Sincerely,

General George S. Patton

Speedy and Bill stood there, dumbfounded, without saying a word, as they stared at each other. Finally someone spoke. "You got to be shitting me, he really is a boxer!" said Speedy as his eyes read over the letter once more to make sure he was reading it correctly. "Just a few more weeks and he would have been home free."

Bill looked over Speedy's shoulder so he too could give the letter a second read. He started shaking his head. "Damn his luck," said Bill, scratching his head and getting the tank's thirty weight oil all in his hair. "Well that's a kick in the shorts!"

"What's going on?" said Sleepy as he just got back from a nature call. "Who was that guy in the jeep, and what did he want? What's that you guys are reading?" Neither one spoke as Speedy handed him the letter and turned away. Sleepy's eyes scanned over the note. "Well I'll be. Can you believe it? That just beats all.   He just missed his ticket home."

"Oh he's going home alright," said Bill, "but he will never be the same."

"The hell you say," shouted Sleepy. "You don't know my boy." He turned away from the guys and wiped the tears rolling down his face. "Son of a bitch," he said under his breath and walked away with the letter in his hand as he climbed up into Nellie Bell to be alone. Bill and Speedy didn't say a word to each other; they just got back to the task at hand and fixed the oil leak.

"I'm so sorry Pete," said Sleepy as he once again read over Patton's letter to Pete. He then folded it up and placed it in a shoebox he had hidden under his seat for safe keeping in old Nellie Bell.

Chapter 19

She's a Keeper

"CIGARETTE?" SAID PETE, TRYING TO BE ROMANTIC, as he looked deep into Millie's eyes. Millie was the girl he ran over at the foot of the stairs at the USO club a couple of weeks earlier. And now through hard work and perseverance, Pete finally convinced her to a date, or at least to see him again.

"No thank you soldier and you, you, you, shouldn't smoke those old nasty things either." Millie pushed the cigarette away from her face.

"What are you a doctor?"

"No, I'm, I'm, a nurse, so I can tell you those things are, are, bad for you."

"Smoking ain't bad. Heck, the army gives us the things," said Pete holding up a green pack of Lucky Strike.

"Yeah, they sent you to war too, Einstein," replied Millie as they both laughed.

"You got a good point," Pete agreed and threw the cigarette on the ground. The two sat in the Willys jeep under a grove of big beautiful oak trees on the outskirts of town for a longest time without speaking. They both knew they didn't have to say a word; they liked each other right off from the first night they met. Pete reached over and held her hand and looked deep into her blue eyes.

"What do you do?" asked Millie to break the ice of silence.

"Me, I drive a tank in the 7th Army for General George S. Patton."

"No, silly, in real life, back home, before, all, all this crazy war stuff?" Millie asked as she moved a little closer to Pete in the jeep.

"Oh, back home I worked as a grocery manager in a warehouse," Pete said in a low voice sounding not too proud. "Pretty much a dead end job, it pays the bills. But on the weekends I fight," Pete said with enthusiasm, as he explained to Millie his love for boxing and his hopes that someday he will be a contender. He told her of his family and Uncle Lou and his boxing story. Millie sat there listening intently to his every word. Pete hadn't talked this much in one sitting in his whole life. Millie was so easy to talk to, and he knew then she was special as he looked up to the stars in the night sky. "It sure is peaceful out here. Nobody would know a war is going on would they?"

"No they wouldn't," Millie agreed as she moved a little closer to Pete. "Not till they saw all the soldiers and tanks and guns," Millie said with a laugh.

Pete knew now was the time and he turned and once again he was stopped by her beautiful eyes. He then reached over and kissed her long and hard. They both enjoyed it. He kissed her again till Millie stopped and tried to think of something else, before it was too late to stop, and was afraid of what would happen if she let it go any further.

"Hey, hey, soldier. Don't get fur, fur, fresh with me. You better take me home, big boy." She quickly pulled away from Pete, and sat up straight in the Willy's, pretending she was not at all interested in Pete and started to fix her hair a little.

Pete just smiled. He knew she liked him. Pete put the jeep in gear and they drove off down the small road of Sicily on their way to Palermo, back to Millie's W.A.C.K unit. The two didn't talk for the longest time, till Pete broke the ice. "Sorry about that back there," shouted Pete as the wind poured over their bodies while the jeep bounced and rattled its way down and over the old dirt road. "Sorry about kissing you back there," said Pete.

"That's OK, I mean, yeah you should be," Millie replied with a smile on her face. Pete saw her smile and knew he was in the clear so he slowed the jeep down to take their time getting back to the base.

Then with a flash and a bang, out of nowhere came an explosion that rocked the jeep almost off the road as Pete fought with the steering wheel to keep from wrecking the speeding vehicle. Millie screamed from the sound of the explosion that landed straight ahead in front of them. She then screamed once again when she saw the army truck that had just been hit by the same explosion lying on its side. There were flames and bodies everywhere. It was a troop carrier that was been hit by a mortar shell or land mine. Pete quickly checked out the scene to see if the attack was over. He looked at Millie and ordered her to stay in the jeep as he checked out the situation with the truck.

"Stay here? Heck I'm the nurse!" she said, as she grabbed the first aid kit out of the jeep, and the two took off to help. Once again a second flash and another bomb exploded, but the two were too far in to stop their advice now.   The second bomb was well off its mark and Pete and Millie kept advancing with caution. Once they got to the truck they saw several boys lying hurt. A couple of men were unconscious with flames all around them. Pete grabbed the two men and pulled them out of harm so Millie could attend to them.

"Oooh please help," cried out a soldier raising his arm as he saw Pete and Millie coming to the rescue.

"Quick help this one," said Pete to Millie as he pulled a soldier out of the truck and drug him over to the side of the road with one hand, holding onto his neck with the other, trying to stop the bleeding. The other soldiers that were not hurt started to return fire as gun fire broke out from the American soldiers around the truck. They seemed to be shooting back at no one in the dark and no one returned the fire. Millie rushed over and quickly started making bandages as she instructed a soldier to apply pressure to the man's wounded neck. Pete got the rest of the men out of the wrecked troop carrier before they heard a loud bang and a flash as the truck exploded in flames.

"Stop, stop, hold your fire!" shouted Lieutenant Donald Mc George who was the officer in charge. They finally realized no one was there to shoot at and the firing was stopped. Slowly the men started getting the area in order, grouping up and attending to the wounded and grabbing anything that seemed important. They then tried to move to what seemed to be a safer spot on higher ground. All the while Pete and Millie stayed, working tirelessly on the wounded.

" Where in the world did you two come from, heaven?" said the Lieutenant as he walked over to the two.

"We were on the road just behind you sir," said Millie as she worked hard on her patient without looking up at him, trying to stop the bleeding by applying pressure to his wounds.

"It's our first date," said Pete looking up at the Lieutenant with a smile you couldn't wipe off.

"Well I say she's a keeper," said the Lieutenant.

"Just doing my job sir," said Millie she moved over to work on another soldier in pain.

"Well, thank God you two were nearby is all I can say," and patted both of them on the shoulder. With that, the Lieutenant walked off to call once again to headquarters, making sure help for his men would arrive soon.

Several hours later Pete and Millie made their way back to base. The two just sat there in silence as their minds were going over what had just happened. They were covered with from head to toe black and dirty from the battlefield and totally exhausted as they set in the jeep trying to catch their breath.

"It must have been a small band of Germans on patrol. It happens all the time," said Pete.

"Not to me, remember. I'm a nurse, not a real soldier."

"You were pretty good out there today," said Pete as he lay back in the jeep smoking a cigarette. They had parked in front of Millie's barrack.

"You weren't that bad out there yourself," said Millie as she reached over and grabbed the cigarette from Pete's mouth and took a draw from the Lucky Strike herself.

Pete sat up in his seat as he watched Millie take a drag of the cigarette. "I thought you said …," started Pete on Millie's stand on smoking.

"I said it was bad for you. I,I,I, didn't say I haven't done it before," replied Millie.

"I understand. It's been a hell of a night. Wish we had something stronger."

"You can say that again," she said as she leaned over and pulled a small flask out from between her legs. "Thank goodness for garter belts," she laughed. The two kissed as she got out of the jeep. "Thanks for the date Soldier. You, you, you, sure know how to show a girl a good time."The two then took a small drink from her flask.

The sun was just coming up over the horizon as Pete drove his jeep back to his camp. With a smile on his face and remembering the Lieutenant's words he said to himself out loud, "she's a keeper."

Chapter 20

Physical Therapy

WALTER REED MEDICAL CENTER was one of the largest Army hospitals in the world, and at the time in World War II it was called Walter Reed General Hospital, named after Major Walter Reed, an Army physician that led a team of doctors who confirmed that yellow fever was transmitted by mosquitoes, not by direct contact with someone.

These were dark days for Pete, trying to cope with the loss of his leg plus the fact he would never box again. Month after month Pete struggled with both the mental issues and the daily task of painful physical therapy. Pete lay in the bed thinking of back home. He was in Washington D.C. at a great hospital but that was still a long way from Hopedale he thought. The Army had kept up with Pete's whereabouts to his folks back home so they knew he was alive and safe, but Pete never once called or wrote them. He was trying to come to grips with the situation as it was getting harder to deal with the closer he was from being released from the hospital. Being a cripple was a world he could not bear. How would you work in a warehouse on crutches, much less fight again? His world as he knew it was over. Where to now? "Where do we go from here?" Pete whispered to himself.

"Hey big boy ready to take a ride?" asked Kevin, the orderly with the wheelchair and a smile on his face. Pete, with his back to him, did not move. "Come on man. I ain't got all day daddy, day light's burning," he said.

Kevin was a great kid from Alabama and was stationed at Walter Reed since the war started. He had seen his share of broken bodies and all kinds of pain. But he was good at his job and the doctors and nurses respected him highly.

"All right, this is your last time white boy. You either get in this wheel chair or I'm going to pour this here bed pan all over your white ass," he ordered. Pete turned to see if he had a bed pan in his hand or not; and he did.

"Ok, you don't have to be so dramatic. I'm getting up," Pete said. Kevin laughed as he helped Pete get turned around in the bed and got the wheelchair up close to the bed rail.

"Well, look here, looks like this is going to be a big day for you today Sergeant," said Kevin, as he glanced at the paperwork on his clipboard. "I see here where they're going to fit you for a prosthetic leg." Kevin then applied the brakes to the chair and steadied it for Pete to board his waiting ride.

"That's great," Pete said sarcastically.

"Here you go Sergeant, your chariot awaits," Kevin said still wearing that same big smile he always wore. Pete climbed in the chair and off the two went down the miles of hallways, Kevin talking as they went down the hall. "Now that the war is over we can do nothing but study on getting you well."

"What?" said Pete.

" Yes, you know, the war is over. You can get your mind on the important things, like getting you to walk again".

"What? What did you say about the war?" Pete questioned as he tried to turn around in the chair to see Kevin's face.

"It's over! Didn't you know that man? You must have really been out of it soldier. On both sides, Japan and Europe, that thing is history and so am I if I don't get you to the doctor on time," said Kevin racing down the hall.

"Hey! Do you have to go so fast? I've already lost one leg," Pete said with a laugh and fear in his voice at the same time.

"Hey Orderly, watch out!" shouted a nurse as Kevin came wheeling by, also hitting her as they flew by.

"I can't believe the war is over," thought Pete. Pete looked up just in time to shout watch out as Kevin wheeled the chair on its side going around a corner.

" Oh no," they both shouted as they hit an empty gurney sitting in the hall's intersection and they all ended up on the floor. The wheelchair, patient, and orderly were all lying in a pile.

"Pete," a woman's voice shouted out, "is, is, that you?" said a familiar voice that Pete recognized.

"Millie! Once again we meet on the floor," Pete said.

"Yea, but this, this, time it's not me on top of you," she laughed as she tried to get the two men untangled .

"What in the world are you, you doing here?" she asked, and then she noticed the missing leg. "Oh Pete, I'm so sorry for you." The laughter stopped. She had not seen Pete since the field hospital. He didn't know she saw him that night before he flew off to England.

Pete just looked into her eyes. "Yeah, but I get to see you again," and they kissed and hugged.   Both Kevin and Millie helped Pete back into the chair.

"Are you stationed here?" asked Pete, still staring in her beautiful eyes.

"For now, I was ordered here for just a few weeks to help out with the influx of patients. I,I,I get discharged out of the army in a couple of months. I'll be going back home in,O,O, Ohio. I talked to the hospital there, they still have my old job waiting for me.

"Well you love birds can talk later. Excuse me ma'am but I've got to get the Sergeant here, down the hall to the doctor now. Remember tha's why we wrecked in the first place," said Kevin, as the two hugged and kissed good bye.

"I'll see you soon," said Millie with a tear rolling down her face. Pete reached up and wiped it off.

"Be sure you do," said Pete and off they went.

"Good bye Pete, I love you," she said under her breath as more tears rolled down her face, knowing that might be the last time they would see each other, but not if she could help it.

Chapter 21

Fighting Back

PETE'S PLACE WAS A POOL HALL and a rough place to say the least; it was located in what was called colored town, about half way down Rawhut Street. This was the place where lost souls would show up time to time, and in this stage of Pete's life it was a welcome home to him. Back in the day before the war Pete's was a pretty good place to get a late hour beer or just hang out with your buddies. But the times had changed and the people at Pete's were either hiding out from the police or just hiding. Not a great place for white folks to hang around unless they were looking for trouble and for some reason most the time when Pete and Sleepy showed up, so did trouble. Back from the war with chips on their shoulders, Pete and Sleepy knew for some reason the night would not end without a fight breaking out. Pete Hall, the owner, was always on the guard when those two came through the door, and tonight was no exception.

"Hey Mr. Hall, how's it going tonight?" asked Pete as he placed his crutches against the wall beside the coat rack. Mr. Hall stopped cleaning the beer glass long enough to look to see who walked through the door.

"Damn" he said under his breath. "It was going pretty good. Damn boys, ain't you got somewhere else you can go? I just got the place put back together from the last time." He was hoping against hope they would turn and leave.

The other people in the bar were looking the two white boys over, wondering why they were there as well. The cops had been tough on the folks on Rawhut Street lately and they, too, were white.

"That's no way to talk to a steady customer Mr. Hall," said Pete.

"Now Pete, we all understand you having trouble coming from the war and all, but we don't want no trouble tonight and as far as I can tell you ain't black and black folks around here get a little up tight when a white fellow shows up in an Army uniform . Not to mention the last three times you boys were in here that little friend of yours started another fight." Mr. Hall kept wiping down the bar and watching how everyone was acting with white customers in his place.

"It's not going to be like that again Mr. Hall, I promise," Pete replied.

"Damn, alright, this one time, you two play a couple of games of pool then you two go home right?"

"That's right sir, a couple of games and we are gone," said Pete.

" Ok then, I means it, no fighting boys, not in my place, not tonight," he said.

The black-white thing was never an issue with Pete or Sleepy. The two had worked hand and hand with their black counterparts in the war and both had several friends of color. That wasn't a problem. The problem was Sleepy's mouth and Pete would always stand up for him. Right, wrong or indifferent, Pete would not let Sleepy get hurt. It went back to when they were kids at Dickson's swimming pool, and Sleepy saved Pete from possibly drowning. Mr. Dickson was a mean old man with lots of money and once in awhile he would open his pool up to let the neighborhood children swim. He would charge them, of course. Whatever it was, Pete was the master of arms for Sleepy and Sleepy may have taken advantage of that friendship from time to time. And now, after the war and with Pete losing his leg and drinking pretty heavily, he wasn't ready to back down from any fight. Matter of fact he was most likely looking for one and after about ten beers each, trouble was about to walk in the door at Pete's Pool Hall. His name was 'Johnny Law'.

"Hey which one of you boys parked your car beside the fire hydrant," said Johnny Lomen. The noise of the pool hall stopped and all eyes were on Johnny as he stood at the door leaning on the cigarette machine trying to look cool, combing his oily hair. Lomen was his last name but everyone called him Johnny Law because he loved throwing his weight around like some hot shot cop. No one dared say a word, in fear that the hot head would love to throw you in jail.

Mr. Hall broke the ice and spoke up. "Hey man, ain't nobody in here wrongfully parking out there. We all know the deal."

Johnny jumped forward at Mr. Hall like he was going to hit him. "Shut up old man, ain't nobody talking to your black ass," shouted Johnny. And with that he had everyone's attention, including Pete and Sleepy. The pool hall turned quiet as the whole big room waited for someone to make a move. You could feel the tension and see the mens' hands twist their pool sticks round and round nervously.

Pete reasoned he should do something before someone got killed. "What the hell you trying to do Johnny?" said Pete as he walked around the corner from the back of the pool hall. Johnny was surprised, to say the least, when he saw Pete. It puzzled Johnny to think why white folks were in the pool hall. Johnny was a racist and there was nothing he liked better than to go down Rawhut Street time to time and give the folks down there a hard time; he was a mean son of a gun and a bad cop to boot.

"Hey Pete, didn't know you were in this pool hall with all your new buddies," said Johnny as he looked around the room knowing he better watch what he said.

"I said, what are you doing in here?" Pete asked again, walking ever closer to Johnny.

"Well, you see Pete, I was, I, well you see…" Johnny did not know what to say or do. He was caught red handed giving the folks on Rawhut Street a hard time. He also knew Pete's cousin Dud, who was the Chief of police, and Johnny's boss.

"Yeah, I see you, you son of a bitch, coming down here all white and mighty," shouted Pete, as he started to push Johnny with his pool stick.

"Hey! You can't talk to me like that. I'm an officer of the law."

"You're an ass hole is what you are," said Sleepy, as he stepped out from behind Pete.

Once again Johnny replied back, "You better tell your little midget friend to shut the hell up. I don't care if you are on crutches or not Pete, I'll throw both your asses in jail."

"For what, catching you trying to shake down these nice folks because they aren't the same color as you, red neck?"

"That's it," said Johnny. "You two Nigger lovers are going downtown."

That pretty much did it for the rest of the crowd in the bar. They had taken about enough of Johnny Law and they started to close in on the loud mouth policeman. Pete understood he didn't have much time if Johnny was going to get out of there alive. He watched the crowd of men as they circled around walking closer and closer to Johnny with pool sticks in hand.

"You going to take us downtown, I don't know about all that," said Pete and Johnny started to pull out his gun. With that Pete was through talking and knew he had to move fast. Pete hit Johnny with a right hook and a powerful left cross, so hard he pounded off the pool table before hitting the ground, and he was out like a light. Everybody in the place stood there in shock with their mouths open as Pete got back up and rearranged his crutches. But deep inside everyone loved it, as the cheers broke out, except Mr. Hall.

"Oh my God!" shouted Mr. Hall as he ran out from behind the counter. "Get back everybody, get away from that policeman!" shouted Mr. Hall, making sure the rest of the crowd didn't kill him. Then he turned to Pete, "What have you done now? You are going to bring the whole damn police force down on our ass Pete!" The pool hall was like a bee hive with all the noise and shouting going on. Just then the door opened once more.

"Hold it, shut up! Where is my partner? Has anyone seen my partner?" asked Red Murphy as he walked around one of the pool tables. That's when Red noticed Johnny's body on the floor beside the one of the pool tables and he pulled out his gun. "Nobody moves," said Red as he ran over beside the pool table to check on Johnny's breathing, and found that he was knocked out but alive.

"Everyone against the wall," ordered Red. And the noise level went back up to a fever pitch, everybody shouting and screaming as mayhem was in full force at Pete's Place.

"Hold it, Hold it, hold it Red," shouted Pete as the noise level went down a notch or two. "You need to put up that gun Red, ain't nobody dying around here, Johnny, he'll be ok."

"I said, everybody against the wall," Red ordered for the second time. Pete didn't move, rather he positioned himself beside the radiator pipes and placed his half leg on top so he was well balanced. "I've already called for backup," Red said. "Don't anyone move, I want no trouble out of you people. "

"Oh Lord," cried out Mr. Hall, "I knew something would happen, damn you two crazy white boys."

"Now Red, look here, I can explain," said Pete, as the two stood looking at Johnny asleep on the floor of the pool hall. "Old Johnny here was about to get killed coming down here on Rawhut trying to start something. All I did was save his life by finishing it. That's what happened. These folks were about to send him to his Maker, I'm telling you the truth," Pete demanded. Nevertheless, he knew he was getting nowhere with Red.

"You assaulted an officer of the law Pete and I'm going have to take you and Sleepy in," Red argued.

"Me?" shouted Sleepy in a surprised voice. "Hell fire, I ain't done a damn thing Red.   That Johnny was asking for it and Pete gave it to him like he needed to."

"You can tell all of that to the Judge," replied Red as Johnny was starting to come to. "Hold on partner," said Red as he helped Johnny get up.

"Where is that Pete Smith?" said Johnny with a slight slur.

"I'm right over here sunshine.   How'd you sleep?" Pete asked with a grin.

"Come on Pete, you're coming with us," said Red.

"I don't think so," said Pete, as he threw his crutches on the floor and put his fist up in defense. It was at that same time when other policemen showed up at the pool hall in force. Red had called in an officer down, so the headquarters sent them out as if someone was killed.   They were thinking the worst as they hit the door.

Johnny, seeing the others coming, just looked at Pete and said, "Well Champ, let's see how you do with more than one person." With that he launched himself at Pete. With his knee propped up on the radiator Pete was well balanced and right for the fight that was about to begin. Once again when Johnny got into range Pete let go a powerful blow that sent Johnny back to sleep under the same pool table. Quickly Mr. Hall jumped back behind the counter to hide out, anticipating that all hell was about to break loose. And it did as more of the local customers started to get in the fight. All the while Pete, being propped up by one leg on the radiator heater, was single-handedly fighting off a large amount the police force. As he was being attacked, one by one Pete sent those policemen flying. Pete was back in form with each left cross, right hook, jabbing left, left, then that crunching right again. There was literally a pile of policemen at Pete's foot. All the time Sleepy kept howling instructions like they were back in the ring.

   Not to be left out, the rest of the folks in the bar started taking up for Pete as they too were getting into the act. It was a free-for-all, with pool balls and chairs flying through the air and pool sticks being used as clubs to battle off night sticks. And as bodies flew, the pool table lights being hit cast an eerie strobe light effect as the long and short shadows caused the silhouettes of fighters to dance all around the room. Mr. Hall would occasionally crane his neck out from under the bar to see and note the destruction of his beloved bar.

   The police had their hands full as everyone seemed to enjoy what they all felt to be a wonderful payback to police abuse. Sleepy would pop up, hit a policeman and quickly ducked back under the closest pool table, and would periodically grab a policeman's leg and pull him down for a cheap shot with a beer bottle. There were beat-up cops lying on the floor everywhere, but more reinforcements were called in to the police station and the steady flow of more cops was endless. The pool hall looked like a saloon scene out of an old western movie. Pete sat back and waited till the next victim was in range and again he would strike with a heavy blow. One by one each cop looked as if he was sent in to be slaughtered. But the years had paid its toll on Pete and he was long from the ring, and was not the fighter of old, soon beginning to tire. After what seemed to be hours the police finally bull rushed him and got the upper hand. They finally took control of Pete and soon the whole mob, and just like that he and Sleepy and the whole gang of civil right protesters were hauled off to jail. In 1947 the sweeping tide of change of race had come. But not on a bus in Alabama or at a nearby lunch counter in Greensboro. That would be much later in American history. No, it had started years before all that in hundreds of small towns all over the southern states in places like Pete's Place, and Rawhut Street and the nation would never be the same.

Chapter 22

One Punch Brown

"PEANUTS ! GET YOUR HOT PEANUTS, "shouted Aileen, as she worked through the crowd selling her goods once again on fight night at the city hall. And tonight the place was packed with fight fans to see a good one; on the card was Pete Smith, "the Hopedale Homicidal," and "One punch" Guy Brown.

"That will be five cents sir," said Aileen as she handed the fresh bag of hot nuts to a waiting customer. She then looked up and saw Lou and Pete entering the ring along with Sleepy, a cigar in the corner of his month and water bucket in his hand. The crowd laughed as Sleepy dropped the bucket trying to get in the ring and down poured the whole bucket of water down onto the reporter's desk getting the group of guys pretty wet. To make matters worse, he jumped down and tried to quickly clean up his mess, knocking over tables, lamps, drinks and microphones.

"Get the hell out of here you fool," said E.Z. Jones, the manager of the local radio station WBBB.

"Get off of us, get out of the way!" shouted a mad reporter from the

Times- News paper.

Aileen laughed too as she watched the mayhem unfold, but her eyes never lost sight of Pete. She wanted to hug him so badly and wish him good luck, but it was show time now and Pete had nothing but this fight on his mind. Sleepy now recovered from his mishap and was on the ready with a full bucket of water and dry towels. Lou looked out over the large crowd as he stood in the corner of the ring counting heads, knowing that he would get a cut of the house ticket sells. He then started working on Pete, checking on his gloves again and giving him a last minute speech.

"Ok Pete, remember what I taught you, but try not to think too much."

"I won't Lou."

"Let your body react, it's all second nature now."

"Ok, yes sir."

"Go out there and make quick work of this guy, and watch out for that right hook, it's dangerous."

"Quick work, I understand Uncle Lou."

"You understand me Pete? You need to make fast work of this fella."

"Will do Uncle Lou," Pete said as he stood up and backed off the stool and stood beside the ropes in his corner waiting for the referee to signal the men to meet in the center of the ring for the prefight instructions. And waiting in the other corner was Keosey "Guy" Brown, known as one punch Guy. Brown was a real crowd pleaser and an all round good fighter. Fighting nearly every week, he would rack up over 340 fights before he retired from the ring. He was coached by the legendary Ebb Gantt. Lou knew all too well about these two from the Charlotte and Gastonia area. He also knew Pete was ready to clean the slate and start anew, he really wanted redemption after that Hard Rock fight. Now, with Lou training him a new style, and new attitude, Pete was ready, as the house light went down and ring lit up. The two met in the center of the ring for their pre-fight instructions from the referee, Tommy Dickson.

"Ok gentlemen, I want a clean fight tonight. You understand no biting, no galling, or hitting from behind, or below the belt. If someone gets knocked down the one standing must go to the neutral corner and wait for my instructions. Do you two understand?" Both men shook their heads in agreement." Do you have any questions? Alright then, I want you two to shake hands and let's come out fighting."

The two men went back to their respective corners, disrobed and applied their mouthpieces, all the while shaking their arms and legs, and craning their necks back and forward to loosen up and be ready to fight. The hall became electric with the anticipation of a good fight.

The bell rings and quickly the two meet and start feeling each other out with a couple of jabs here and there. Pete started working on the new style of jabbing with his right, not the left. This was new to both he and Brown. Brown thought he was going to be fighting a right hander, not a south paw. And to beat Brown, Pete knew he had to move fast. Brown tried to be the aggressor by pushing and trying a couple of jabs on his own, working on the body with solid hard punches to Pete's mid section all along directing Pete to the corner of the ring. Realizing his tactic, Pete was thinking that's not a place you want to be. So Pete started to counter his move with some hard jabs and hooks and doing some directing of his own. This seemed to work and Pete was easily directing and pushing Brown where he wanted him to go with some hard lefts and right combinations. It looked like Brown was finding himself studying on Pete's new south paw style, more than the fight itself. Watching Pete's every move Guy Brown found himself in the corner of the boxing ring. There was no way out except through Pete.

Then out of the blue, Pete let out a tremendous left hook that caught Brown completely flat footed. He bounced off the ring ropes and down in a pile he went after one shot! The crowd was in shock, as the referee's counting began. Brown didn't move a muscle, he was out cold.

"One, Two, Three," Tommy Dickson shouted the count! The crowd was on their feet keeping count with the ref in unison," four, Five, six."

"Move Pete, go to the corner," Lou instructed. Pete could not believe it himself as he went to the opposite corner of the ring.

"Lou's new left handed style works," Pete was thinking, "and what a left-handed punch indeed, it was a hay maker from downtown," he thought.

Lou and Sleepy were jumping up and down in the corner; they couldn't believe what they just saw, as the referee and the entire crowd reached ten in their count and the fight was over. "One punch" Guy Brown was on the receiving end of Pete's one tremendous punch, and this time he was the receiver of the punch. The fight was less than one and half minutes and Keosey Guy Brown was sent packing as he was slow to get up from the ring's canvas. Lou ran to the center of the ring and with a big hug he embraced his nephew as the referee raised Pete's arm as the victor.

"That a boy Pete! You did it! He didn't know what hit'em," shouted Lou. "You just took down one of the best fighters in the business," he added.

"No, we did, it took all of us," said Pete. "I don't know where that punch came from, but thank God for you, Uncle Lou. You are the best Lou," said Pete as he walked over to check on the condition of Guy Brown who was still sitting on his backside, but was ok.

"Heck of a punch kid," said Brown as he set there dazed and confused and shaking out the cobwebs, as his handlers and manager ran over to check on their boy.

"What did I tell you Lou, that a boy Pete!" shouted Aileen as she threw down the peanuts and jumped up onto the ring. They all three hugged again and left the ring. And another Friday night fight was over with Pete Smith, the "Hopedale Homicidal" being victorious once again.

The crowd now was all gone. Pete and Lou were headed to the car as Sleepy went back inside to gather up a couple of things he had forgotten.

"Hold it right there short stuff," said Dud as he looked down at all the water on the floor around the reporter's desk.

"What?" said Sleepy. "That was an accident, besides its water, it ain't going to hurt nobody.

"Look here stumpy, our boy might have won the fight tonight, but this is still City Hall and I would like for you to clean up your mess proper, you understand?" and with that Dud pulled open his coat wide enough to show Sleepy his police badge.

"Dud, we all know you're the new police chief, everybody knows that," said Sleepy as he started to get down on his hands and knees to mop up the water with the towel he had wrapped around his neck. Slowly he started sopping up the water as he looked back to see if Dud had walked off or not.

"He's an asshole," said Sleepy under his breath and shaking his head as he watched Dud walk out of the large hall and knowing no one could hear him. The only sound was that of the light switch, as one by one the lights were being turned off. Sleepy kept shaking his head and cleaning up the water in the dark, but he had a smile on his face, as he said to himself, " we won."

Chapter 23

The Phone Call

" I DON'T CARE WHAT YOU SAY, IT'S MY RIGHT, I get to use the phone, I get one call," shouted Pete as he was arguing with a police officer early Saturday morning in the jail house at the police Department. Pete demanded, "I know my rights I tell you."

"You don't know shit," said Officer Sam Ivey. "You get one phone call only if I or your cousin says so and not before."

"You better let me have that call or I'll …." Pete stopped talking when he saw the door open.

"You'll do what Champ?   Beat me up too?'' said Dud as he came walking down the hall to the jail cell. Pete sat back down and wondered what to do or say. "Hey lookie here, all dressed up in his Army uniform to boot. Look like the Army would not let someone as messed up as you wear their uniform."   Dud kept giving it to Pete and Pete sat there and took it. "Looks like Aunt Knobby and Uncle Jim are going to get their hearts broken again when you call them this morning. I told you time and time again you needed help; well this phone call is the only help you'll get from me. And this time let them know who let you have that call," said Dud. He stopped talking and looked in at Pete for the last time. "Damn you're a hard headed S.O.B. You're lucky you weren't killed."

Pete turned to Dud. "Me? Why don't you ask your fine officers who feels like the lucky ones," said Pete with a smile on from ear to ear.

"I'm the Chief of Police damn it. You don't talk to me that way. Family or not, I'll wipe that smile off your ass," and Dud reached in like he was going to hit Pete. Pete just laughed as Dud stormed off, talking under his breath. Pete stood up in the cell and looked at Officer Ivey.

"Ok boss, you heard the man. Let's have that phone call."

Ivey looked at Pete. "Sure thing Buddy, soon as I get all the paperwork completed," and he too walked off. Pete realized he was not in charge now and sat back down to wait. It was all he could do under the circumstances.

"What now?" asked Sleepy after hearing all the conversation that went on between Pete, Dud, and Officer Ivey.

"Shut up Sleepy. Shit will hit the fan soon enough."

As the morning sun arose so did Chief Dud Matheson. Making his way down the steps for breakfast he asked his wife for the newspaper with his coffee like he did everyday but this day was different. He kissed his wife Carolynn good morning and started to open the paper.

"Darling don't you want to go outside and get some fresh air this morning? It's beautiful," said Carolynn with a strange look on her face.

"What is it?" Dud asked.

"Nothing dear, I thought you might want to go outside before you read the paper. You know, go look at the beautiful world that God has given us." Dud knew right then something was wrong. He knew his wife like a book. He quickly grabbed the paper, and there it was in bold print. .. **Police Attack Unarmed Amputee Veteran,** plus a photo of Pete in the jail cell. The photo was of him holding himself up by the bars because he had only one leg, plus, that's right, wearing his Army uniform.

"O' my God," shouted Dud, "that son of a bitch! He has done it now. He didn't call Aunt Knobby at all; he called the damn newspaper reporters, "as he threw the paper down on the table.

"Now dear, you know your blood pressure, you need to calm down," Carolynn said in a soft voice.

"Calm down? That cousin of mine just made me the laughing stock of the whole town! Damn him to hell!" Dud fell back in his chair with a look of disgust on his face.

"Dud," Carolynn shouted, this time in a loud voice. "Don't you think that boy has been to hell and back? He needs help. Now, I'm sure you can find a way out of this, you always do." Dud shook his head again knowing it was time he headed up the stairs to get dressed. Like it are not he had to go in town and face the music. He stood up, leaned over and kissed Carolynn on the top of her head, as if to say you are right. He then turned and headed up the stairs to start his journey.

The newspaper folks had started to gather outside of the police station when Dud arrived. He walked passed them without saying a word. "Hey, hey Chief, over here! Are we locking up war heroes now! Do you want to give a statement?" they asked. Dud was all business, not saying a word to the reporters, and marched up the front steps of the jail house and kept walking straight to the cell where Pete was waiting.

Seeing Pete Dud started shouting. "OK you smart ass, you got your laugh. Now here's the deal. I don't care what the hell is going on in that screwed up mind of yours, and don't want to know. I do know life must be hard on you with the leg and all. But the bottom line is you assaulted my police force. Hell, I got three men in the damn hospital Pete. But I also know Johnny, and I know you two hate each other. So there's a good chance he most likely did start it, I understand. So here's the deal, you and your midget friend here will get the hell out of my jail cell on one condition." Pete and Sleepy were all ears as the two stood up in the jail cell. "You two will not talk to the newspaper reporters, radio, TV or even your friends about this, I mean nobody. Look at me!" he shouted. "Do you two understand me?" he asked again. Both guys shook their heads yes. "Ok then, I'll talk to the judge and we will act like this thing never happened," said Dud.

"Deal," said both Pete and Sleepy.

Dud turned to the jailer. "Ivey get them out of here through the back way, and be sure you wait till the newspaper folks have left." Dud then turned back around to Pete and looked him straight in the eye. "One other thing Pete," said Dud as he stepped closer to the bars. "If you don't get help, and I mean go to a mental health hospital, like Camp Butner or Dix Hill to get some mental help, I don't want to ever see you or talk to you again, ever. Family or no family, I mean it. If you don't get some help soon you are going to kill your damn self."

Pete never got the chance to talk. He and Sleepy just stood there and took their whipping and watched Dud as he walked down the hallway to his office.

"And all we tried to do is help keep his men from getting killed and this is the thanks we get."

"Shut-up Sleepy, just shut, up," said Pete as he sat back down on the small bed in the cold jail cell, wishing things were different between he and Dud and knowing he was wrong and Dud was right. He pushed his back up against the wall, and in disgrace he put both hands to his face.

He was ashamed of himself, now that he had hit bottom.

It would be many years before Pete and Dud would ever speak to each other again.

Chapter 24

Easy to Track

JIM SMITH WAS SITTING on the back porch of the house smoking his pipe, enjoying the morning air, as he watched the birds fly overhead. The sun was rising over the small home that they all lived in. It was given to him by the mill he worked for. He and his family had moved to Hopedale from Erwin, North Carolina to become the new plant manager at Carolina Mills, years ago. Big Jim was a hard man to live with and his employees would agree that he was a pretty tough man all together. Pete also had tough times with his dad and the two did not always see eye to eye. Even though Pete was a boxer, he was smart enough to know you don't mess with Big Jim. He was a God fearing man and he would beat the God in or out of you, either way he didn't care. And Pete was on that receiving end of his belt many a time. But now, since Pete had returned from war and his hospital time was behind him, Big Jim was a different man. It was a good guess time and getting closer to meeting your maker has its way of chilling folks out and in this time of Big Jim's life he tried to see things differently, maybe a little more understanding, maybe. The milk truck drove off after delivering the milk to the house and the driver tooted his horn and waved at Pete when he saw him walking down the dirt road in front of his home. Pete let go of the handle to one of his crutches as he too waved back at the milkman and made his way down the drive to the back of the house, hoping to get inside before anyone saw him sneak in the backdoor.

"Hey Dad, I didn't see you there," said Pete, as he rounded the corner of the house with a surprised look on his face.

"Well hey there yourself. Funny to see you up this time of day. You sure are up pretty early."

" Well you know me Dad, I like to get up early and see what's going on in the world." Pete was lying.

"Well son since you're here, maybe we can talk a little bit. Pull up some porch and have a seat."

"Sure Dad, what you want to talk about?"asked Pete as he tucked in his shirt tail and worked his way up the steps to sit in the rocker beside of Jim.

"Actually I was wondering if you are thinking any more about going to Charlotte and working with Lou?"

"You want me to go to work in Uncle Lou's gym? I didn't think you two liked each other very much," Pete said, wondering why his dad all of a sudden wanted him to go to Lou's.

"Well that's not all true," explained Jim. "Lou has stopped drinking for now, and he has a pretty good setup down there in Charlotte.   He is training a bunch of golden gloves and I'm sure he could use the help, and besides that, you love the fight game.   It's in your blood son and they can't take that away from you."

"Yea when I could fight, not like this," Pete said as he looked down at his leg.

"Pete the sport is in your heart, not your leg."

"I understand Dad, but there are a few people I would miss around here."

"Son, it's time for you go and be somebody. You stay here and all you'll do is hang out with that bunch of loser friends of yours and feel sorry for yourself." Jim got up from his rocking chair and turned once again to look at Pete.

"Oh, by the way son, you know Ms. Sally, the pretty lady that lives down the road? You know, the *married* lady down the way?"

"Yea, I know her Dad," said Pete, as his face turned red.

"As you know, her husband is a traveling salesman. And he has been away for a few days and I think today is when he was planning to come home," explained Jim. Pete looked at his dad with a puzzled look on his face.

"And what does that have to do with anything Dad?"

" Well you see son, you are still a young man, and it looks to me that you and Ms. Sally seem to be getting pretty friendly with each other when her husband ain't in town."

Pete again, with a question mark on his face, asked "What does that have to do with me?"

Jim then pointed to the ground where Pete had come from and pointed out the marks that were made by a one legged man on crutches. You could see where they were left in the dirt and along the driveway and along the roadside headed down to Ms. Sally's house.

"Son, it's your business. You are a grown man. You've been to war and hell and back. All I wanted you to know is that you are easy to track!" And with that Big Jim, knowing his life lesson was over; he went back into the house.

Pete just rubbed and shook his head, knowing he was right. "The old man of mine is something."

Chapter 25

Realization

PETE SAT IN THE CHAIR, trying to retrace his hospital moves from Sicily to Walter Reed in Washington, DC. How did he not know the war was over? "Man I must have been out of it," he thought. For the next few days he would read over hundreds of newspapers and ask everyone he met about their accounts of the last few months and year. Pete could not get his fill of stories to fill the blanks from the battle to when he was hospitalized. Those two whole years of nineteen forty three to forty five were a blur to him. He would read all kinds of stories about the death of President Franklin D. Roosevelt, and the new thirty third President of the United States, Harry Truman. He learned how Truman was the one that had ordered the atomic bombing on Japan. The newspapers were full of stories on the deaths of Benito Mussolini and Hitler, and the fall of both Italy and Germany. And the day of all days was August 14th, the day marking the end of War World II, when Japan would finally surrender. Regardless of all the news, the one story Pete still could not believe, was the death of General George S. Patton, killed in a jeep wreck, of all things.

"I met the General one time," said Pete as he and Kevin were working on his physical therapy.

" You did?   Was he a pretty good guy?" Kevin asked as he rubbed and massaged Pete's tendons and muscles in his upper thigh.

"He was ok for a General I guess, pretty much all business when I saw him."

"I bet they got a lot on their minds, those Generals.   Must be tough running an Army, ok Pete turn over so I can work on that back of yours," said Kevin.

"That's for sure; I don't know how they do it," said Pete. "Knowing men are going to die and all, and you being the one sending them out there, must be horrible. I still can't believe a man like that was ended by a car wreck."

" There ain't but so many pages in your book of life," said Kevin. "When your story is over it's over, only the good Lord knows.   Death ain't choosey. Ok I'm done here; I'll see you in the morning."

Pete sat and thought about Kevin's words, knowing he was right, and how lucky he was to have him. "I guess God is looking out for me," he said under his breath.

Day after day those two read the newspapers and spoke of the years that Pete forgot. There was a story on Bert Shepard, a one legged pitcher that tried out for the Washington Senators baseball team. He, too, lost his leg in the war. In college basketball that year DePaul won the NIT and George Mikan scored 34 points. In baseball the Detroit Tigers beat the Chicago Cubs in the World Series. It had taken almost a full year for Pete to recover from the brain trauma he received from that minefield. Kevin, the orderly, and Pete would talk for hours about lost time and they, in turn, became good friends for life.

"You telling me that we have a bomb that can blow up a whole city?" Pete said with a question in his voice.

"No we had two cities blown up, the whole damn town, both are gone."

"Why didn't we blow up Germany?" Pete asked.

"Didn't need to, they quit already. The Japs were a little more hardheaded. So we had to show them who was boss. Those Japs are hardhead like you Pete. You must be Japanese!" and they both laughed. "I can't believe you don't know this stuff."

As the weeks and months went by Pete was getting stronger and working on his crutches pretty good but the artificial leg was a different story.

"Pete, we have to get you to put more weight on that leg or you ain't ever going to walk," said Kevin.

"Leg, hell! I don't have much of any leg there. It's a nub, that's all. "Pete sat , rubbing the end of his leg.

"Well, that's all we have to work with, 'cause it damn sure ain't growing back," said Kevin as he helped balance Pete between the hand rails, trying to walk with the new prosthesis. "We work with what we got in life Pete. Don't start feeling sorry for yourself again. Now, shift your weight on that nub damn it!"

Week after week those two worked on getting Pete back to walking on two feet. They tried everything but the leg did not fit right and would make Pete's leg incredibly sore for days. One morning Kevin came in Pete's ward with a big smile on his face you could not wash off. He had been working on Pete's prosthesis.

  "Boy you sure look happy. What's going on? Is it your birthday or something?" Pete was curious of Kevin's behavior.

  "Now try that," Kevin said, as he handed Pete his prosthetic limb. Pete turned his leg in the direction of his nub and slid on the prosthetic and stood up on both feet in front of his bed. "Wow that feels great!" Pete announced as he walked around the room getting a better feel of his new appendage. "It doesn't rub like the old one did. In fact it doesn't hurt at all. Where did you get the leg Kevin? Did you steal somebody's leg? Please tell me you didn't."

  "I didn't get or steal nothing, that's your old leg; I just took it home the other night and worked on it myself in my workshop. That thing was rubbing blisters on that nub so bad, I just scooped out a little more wood and put a hatband inside so your weight would be riding on that band and not rubbing on the wood at the end. That will give you more support I think."

  "All I know is it works," said Pete, as he marched around the room like never before. "Thanks Kevin, you're the best."

  "Don't thank me. It was my father-in-law's hat band, so do me a favor and don't tell him!"

Chapter 26

Gym Rat

CHARLOTTE, NORTH CAROLINA was the hot spot of the southern boxing world in those days. Located near the state line of both the Carolinas, Charlotte was where the kids from the south who wanted to be somebody in the boxing game went. And Lou's gym was the point of the spear. Lou was a big name in the fight game and Lou handpicked most of the talent. Others just showed up in hopes that Lou would take an interest in them, which would surely help out their careers. These were boys from all walks of life and not all from the best side of the tracks. Some were downright dangerous but mostly misguided street kids. This didn't matter to the big hearted Lou. Lou could see talent and even if that kid didn't have any boxing ability Lou wanted try to help in any way he could. Lou was a rough but kind man who was like a father figure to a lot these boys. And they respected him as well.

"Pete get me some water over here boy," shouted a boxer named Randy, standing beside the ring working on his head gear.

"Hell no Pete, you come over here like I said about twenty minutes ago and help me get off these gloves," said another.

"Hold on fellows. I'll be there in a minute," said Pete, picking up towels and trying to do ten things at once. The gym was full of fighters trying to make a name for themselves. All these young men were thinking they were better than the other, wanting to be the next Rocky Marciano or Joe Louis. Pete was there to help out his Uncle Lou and between the two they were making this one of the best gyms in the Carolina's.

"Hey Pete, why do you let those assholes talk to you like that?" asked Tom O'Leary, one of Lou's business partners that just happened to come by that afternoon when Lou was out on errands. There was just something about this guy Pete didn't like. And he was always around when Lou was not.

"Oh, they don't mean anything by it. They're just young kids; a couple of poundings in the ring will straighten those boys right up."

"You're a better man than me. I don't know how you take it," said Tom, as Lou walked in.

"Hey what you doing here Tom?" asked Lou. "I told you I'll get your money."

"Now hold off, Lou I'm not here on business. I just wanted to come by and check on things."

"Yea right. I know a couple of guys you have already checked on. Now get out!" Lou shouted and everyone in the place looked over as they heard Lou's loud voice.

"Ok Champ I'm going. It was nice talking to you Pete," and like that Tom was gone. Pete turned and looked at his Uncle.

"What was that all about?" said Pete. "I thought you two were business partners."

"Yea he wants to be in my business," said Lou. "Look Pete, there's all kinds of folks in the fight game and most are bad people. It's a tough life. Look I'll be in my office if you need me." Lou then turned and walked off across the gym to his office.

"Hey nubby, I said I wanted some water," said Randy, talking to Pete. Pete kept working and waited a few seconds before he turned to see who was calling out the insult. When he saw it was Randy he laughed.

"Who you calling Nubby? Hell we've all seen you in the showers," laughed Pete. Everyone that heard him laughed as well which made Randy madder. Pete started cleaning up the gym again like nothing was going on.

"Hey fellow you don't turn away from me when I'm talking to you," shouted Randy , really pissed as he started walking over to Pete.

"What do you think you are, a great Pugilist?" said Pete, seeing Randy coming over, and knowing something was about to happen. Pete stopped and placed his knee in the seat of a folding chair near the ringside. Randy never noticed.

"Don't you curse me, I'm talking to you," said Randy as he put his left hand on Pete's shoulder. Pete turned and quickly ducked as the first punch of Randy's went sailing by his ear. Pete balanced on the chair and caught Randy with a combination of a left hook and a right cross, right in the mouth. Even with head gear on Randy was out cold. No one could believe that the wash boy knocked out Randy and of course they did not know Pete's background. With all the noise going on in the gym Lou quickly came running out of his office. Then he saw Pete standing over Randy, checking to see if he was alright.

"Ok everybody, get back to work, the fun is over," Pete said and he tried to get Randy to his feet. Lou shook his head in disbelief and with a laugh, turned and went back in his office, knowing he had the right guy working for him now. He's going to work out fine, Lou thought to himself.

Chapter 27

Dreams

THE LANDSCAPE WAS DARK, and the fog was rolling in once again as Pete lay in the muddy field of corn. The cold and dark was all around him as his mind wondered about his circumstances. The moon was full again and the clouds close to the ground, moving really fast as the wind picked up speed. Pete then heard a sound of corn stalks breaking and rustling in the wind. The sound ushered in dark figures approaching. As they got closer they all looked familiar. They were guys from his platoon and outfit, the seventh army.

"Hey Pete, get up! Let's go," said Howard Isley. "The Germans are right behind us. You got to move, get up!" he shouted as he kept on walking right by Pete back into the darkness of the corn field. Then Pete called out his name.

"Howard Isley is that you?" shouted Pete, as he thought … that can't be, Howard was right beside me. He was killed on the road when the patrol was ambushed, and I saw it happen. What is going on? Then another soldier from the same outfit walked by Pete, and then another. It was like he was in a bus station full of friends, but he wasn't. He was still in the cornfield of the damned. One by one Pete watched as they all walked off into the dark and away from him. Then silence, not a sound to be heard and the moon that was so bright a minute ago had now vanished as well, leaving a dark, black world all around him. Minutes passed, which seemed like hours, and then the silence is broken by a voice.

"Are you ok?" a voice rang out, but it was not Howard this time. Pete turned to look up as best as he could to see, but there was nobody in his line of sight, just the darkness. He wrestled down in the dirt and mud to cover himself like a blanket and to hide from his fear.

Again the voice, "Stay right there. We will get you," the voice cried out again. Pete was thinking he was saved. Then he thought "Oh shit, No, don't!" He heard the blast and screams, and he heard it again and over and over and over, it would not stop. It was the noise of landmines going off over and over as the sound repeated itself. The noise was so deafening Pete's screams could not be heard in the cornfield. He looked over to his left and saw more men from his platoon and they too were walking by Pete as the bombs were going off. One by one he watched as they were blown right out of their boots, directly in front of where Pete was laying. He tried to close his eyes but they would not shut. He then tried to cover them, but his arms would not move. He was trapped and forced to watch as the carnage unfolded.

Over and over the sounds of explosions repeated till the screams from Pete were heard all over the gym. Lou woke up and ran down the hall where Pete was sleeping. "Pete, Pete, wake up," Lou said as he was shaking him to wake up. Pete then opened his eyes and saw Uncle Lou standing over him in the darkness of his little room in back of the gym. "You were dreaming again. Are you ok son?"

Pete awoke with his eyes wide open, sweat pouring out of his skin; his sheets were soaked with perspiration. "What, yeah, oh Lou, I'm ok Lou," Pete said as Lou was shaking him to wake up. Hundreds of nights it seems Pete has played out those hours of hell laying in that cornfield in Italy with those poor souls trying to rescue him over and over, till once again he awakes in a flop sweat of tears and pain. "Sorry Lou. I am fine. It's just one of those dreams again." Pete was wondering if he would ever forget that horror. "I just don't understand why and when they come, looks like they would get tired of trying to rescue me by now."

"Maybe that's the problem," said Lou. " Maybe your medics can't stop until they do rescue you, one way or another. Now go back to sleep. We got a lot of work to do today."

Pete watched as Lou walked off down the hall and started thinking of the words Lou just said. Pete then reached under his bed and pulled out a bottle of Old Crow whiskey and took a big swig of 'who hit John'. "Damn those dreams," he sighed and took another gulp, then placed it back in its resting place.

"Ok ghost, just let me sleep a couple more hours," and with that Pete rolled over and closed his eyes.

Chapter 28

Gone like the Wind

THE TWO MEN WERE SHOUTING IN A DARK ALLY. One had his hands around the other's neck, while the other was lying on the ground in the alley behind the gym.

"Look here you broken down old man. Frank Palermo wants his money and if you don't come up with it soon this gym, plus your dumb ass, may just go up in flames. You understand me?" said Tom. Lou nodded his head in understanding as he watched Tom and a couple of his goons get in his car and drive off.

Frank "Blinky" Palermo was an organized crime figure who posed as boxing manager, but was best known for fixing fights. He also ran the City of Brotherly Love's, one of the biggest numbers racket in Philadelphia. Blinky's business partner was Frankie Carbo, a soldier in New York's Lucchese crime family and had been a gunman with Murder,

Inc. These were not good people and Pete knew it and didn't want any part of their kind. Blinky had a stable of boxers under contract, names like Billy "Blackjack" Fox, Welterweight champ Johnny Saxton, Lightweight champion Ike Williams and Welterweight champion, Virgil Akins. He was also notorious for cheating his fighters out of their share of the purses, by hundreds of thousands of dollars.

"Uncle Lou, what the hell was that all about," said Pete, as he ran out the side door down the block to help his Uncle back up on his feet.

"Now, now Pete everything is fine. I just fell down, that's all. I'm ok. You have it all wrong. Tom and I were just having a conversation, that's all."

"Yeah I've had those conversations before but usually it's in the ring. Come on Uncle, what the hell were you two talking about? Or let me put it this way, how much money do you need to pay off this so-called partner?"

Lou was standing there wiping the blood off his mouth and straightening his clothes as he started to talk. "Now Pete don't think that way, you know me."

"Yea, I know you alright. How much Lou?"

"Twenty Gs," Lou said, with his face looking down as he spoke.

"What?" A few seconds went by. "Twenty thousand dollars!" shouted Pete. "Have you lost your mind?"

"But Pete you see…"

"Where the hell are we going to get twenty thousand dollars? Are you kidding me Lou?"

"But Pete, Blinky, wants his money back sooner than I thought. Look son, I've been in a tighter fix than this one before. You just leave it to your old Uncle Lou and we'll be ok."

"Blinky Palermo, the mobster?"

"Yea, but Pete..." Lou could not get a word in. Pete was mad and Lou knew it.

"Blinky Palermo, well hell Lou, why don't you just piss off the whole Lucchese crime family," said Pete. "Blinky Palermo is the most dangerous man in all of boxing! This is just great and getting better as we go. Who else do we owe? Jimmy Hoffa? Are you kidding me? No wonder you drink like a fish. You just got your ass beat up in the back ally and everything is just hunky dory. Are you drunk?"

Pete walked off not believing the situation his Uncle had put them both in. "Blinky Palermo! My God, I guess all the stories of Lou were all true," he thought. And maybe that's the reason everyone wanted Pete to move in and watch over him. But keeping Lou out of trouble was like herding cats.

A few hours later Pete noticed Lou as he stood inside the doorway of Pete's tiny room in the back of the gym. "Is this the maddest you have ever been?" asked Lou. Pete realized Lou was trying to get him to not worry and at that point they both just laughed.

"Ok Lou you win. We will sleep on it, and I'll see you in the morning."

"I love you Pete. It's going to be ok."

Pete tried to be positive as he responded back to his Uncle. "Its fine Lou, I love you too," said Pete.

"Ok then, I'll see you in morning son, "said Lou as he walked down the hall to his room and went to sleep.

The morning came and the gym was a buzz of noise. Pete awoke a little later than usual and he guessed it was because of all thinking he was doing, which made it hard to get a good night's sleep. He still could not believe the situation Lou had put them in. And the worst was about to come as Pete walked into Lou's room.

"Lou, you in here?" he called out to no answer. He looked all over the gym, even in the back ally, but there was no sign of Uncle Lou. He was gone. No wonder he didn't worry, Pete thought. Lou did it again. He could not handle the pressure and like that, he's gone like the wind. "Damn you Lou," Pete said under his breath as he kicked the trash can down the hall to the gym. "What the hell I'm I going to do now?" Pete thought to himself.

"Hey Pete where are the towels?" Randy called out to Pete. With that Pete realized he was not alone. During all the time he was looking for Lou this old building was coming back to life as the boxers and trainers were going through their routine of working on their craft. The big old empty room was now full of life and potential.

"Hell if Lou could do this, I sure as hell could run the thing till he gets back," Pete thought. "We'll just see how it goes," thought Pete as he headed off to get some more towels.

"Hey Pete, where's Lou?   Some guy is looking for him," said Buck Earnhardt, a good kid from Spartanburg and a young boxer with some real promise.

Pete looked over the ring and saw a couple of real rough looking guys standing in the corner. "He stepped out for a little bit. Yeah tell them that and I have no idea when he'll be back."

"Ok Pete, I'll tell them." Buck left with his instructions and told them what Pete said. They were not happy with the news it appeared to Pete. He saw one of the thugs hit the wall with his fist as the two gangsters made their way out of the gym in disgust.

"Well I guess that will hold those clowns off a few days. Now all I got to do is make a little money," said Pete to himself, but how?

Chapter 29

Together Again

"THE GOLDEN GLOVES IS THE NAME given to the winners of the annual competitions for amateur boxers 16 and over," Pete exclaimed as the boys in the gym gathered around to listen to the old ring veteran teach them the craft of boxing. "You see, the national contest is sponsored by the Golden Gloves Association of America. The winners from the regional contest like the ones they have in both cities, Chicago and New York City, has their own regional golden gloves. There are also tournaments such as the intercity Golden Glovers. So when someone says they are a golden glove winner remember that there are many ways they could have received it. But there is only one national winner, called the Golden Glove Tournament of Champions, and each year it is held at a different location. This year it's in Chicago, and I'm going to teach you boys all you'll need to know to get there." As Pete spoke, half a dozen more guys walked up to listen to what Pete had to say about boxing for the golden glove title. Pete loved boxing and nothing gave him more pleasure than being able to pass down his talent and knowledge of the game. Young folks are like sponges. They soak up the information as quick as you give to them if it's something they like. And boy these kids could not get enough from Pete. They loved him, maybe not all of them, but most.

"Ok Pete, I got another question," said Randy, looking about half pissed off.

"What is it?"

"What was that word you cursed me with the other day?"

"Cursed at you? No way did I curse at you Randy. I sometimes want to however," and Pete laughed and so did everyone else in the crowd.

"Yeah you did. It was pig- or –ist, pug or is…. or something like that," Randy insisted.

"No, you mean pugilist. That's not a curse word Randy, that's a great word. In fact that's what I want all of you to become. Pugilist is a fancy word that means boxer. The definition of the word is, it's the noble art of fighting with ones fists."

"Is that all, heck I got all mad over nothing," said Randy, as the whole bunch of guys started to laugh at him again.

"That ain't the first time that's happened," said one of the guys in the group.

"Well that's one thing a lot of guys do and that's why you are having a hard time winning in the ring," said Pete. "You guys have to keep your head on straight at all times during the fight. Don't let the other guy get under your skin. You need to turn that anger into speed and precision. And you will need to practice to the point it becomes second nature. And you can recall that nature even when you're so tired you can't think straight. That's when you will be known as a golden glove boxer. Now let's get back to work and turn this place back into a real gym. You never know... there might be a Golden Glover in this bunch." With that everyone grabbed their gloves and mouth piece and headed back to their stations.

The kids really liked Pete, and since Lou left a few years ago he had really turned the place into something special. He had two or three kids with a real chance for golden gloves and a heavyweight boxer in Buck, with a real chance of being a contender.

Pete's leg was really hurting at that point so he turned to head back to his office to attend to it. That's when he heard a voice from the past. "You got room for one more?"

Pete stopped in his tracks; he could not believe it. He knew that voice, and he quickly turned around to see his old friend. "Sleepy!" shouted Pete. The two had not seen each other in years. "For your old, short ass I always have room," said Pete and the two hugged. "Where the hell have you been?"

"I've been to hell and back." said Sleepy. "Lost everything; my house, my wife, my business, everything I once had is gone Pete. I have nowhere to go, so I thought about you."

"You thought right Buddy. This place needs some character. It will be like old times. We'll go out tonight and get a few drinks."

"No, not for me," said Sleepy. Those few drinks got me here in the first place. Ain't no drinking for me anymore."

"I understand. You can watch me down a couple." They both laughed but inside Pete knew he had the same problem. Till this point he just didn't know how handle it. Pete looked at his buddy Sleepy and patted him on the back. "You are not the only one," said Pete. "Ever since I lost my leg I've been fighting that same problem. Now we'll fight through this together."

Sleepy looked at his old friend. He did not have to say a word. He grabbed up his belongings and they both walked down the hall to Pete's office together. And part of the crew of the Nellie Bell was back together again.

Chapter 30

Feast or Famine

THE RAIN WAS POURING DOWN and the traffic stood at a standstill. Pete was stuck in the traffic and was now late to his appointment with the bankers.

"Damn I'm really late," Pete said out loud as he looked for the thousandth time at his watch. "O' hell let them wait," he thought. "It's not like they were giving out samples anyway." But now he was getting tired of just sitting there and the noise of the car horns was getting on his last nerve. Slowly his car inched closer. Pete tried to see what the holdup was as he inched his old Mercury sedan up just a few cars ahead him now. At this point he could start to hear voices and it sounded like someone must have gotten really hurt. His car kept inching up and little by little he could clearly hear the conversation and see the folks involved up there.

The loudest voice was saying, "I'm ok I said, now get your damn hands off of me!" It was an old street bum talking to the police and the crowd in general. Pete looked again in disbelief or was the rain causing the images to be so blurred it was hard to tell who it was.

"No that can't be," Pete thought. The rain was coming down pretty good now and the face of the old man was hard to see at times. For some reason Pete felt drawn to the situation and wanted to help if he could. Pete got out of the car and walked in the direction of the crowd. When he got closer he could not believe his eyes and he was speechless. Pete stood with his mouth opened in shock. Pete did not have the say a word, but the old man did.

"Say Pete, could you please tell this S.O.B. that I'm fine so we can get the hell out of here."

Pete could not believe what he was seeing. The old bum in this wild scene was none other than Uncle Lou himself. This was his uncle, a man whom Pete had not seen or heard from in over twenty years. He had thought for years he was truly dead. Now, out of the blue in the middle of a downtown traffic intersection between walk and don't walk, there he was in all his glory.

"Buster," Lou shouted. "Someone get my dog. Where the hell is Buster?" He shouted several more times.

"Hold on old man, you're not going anywhere," replied an officer. He then turned to Pete. "Sir, do you know this man?"

Pete stood there stunned. "What! Uncle Lou are you kidding me, after all these years, what are you doing here?" Pete was still in shock and at a loss for words. He watched as Lou shuffled toward him and sat along the curbing on the street with the rain still pouring down.

Once again the policeman asked, "Sir, do you know him?"

"Yes I guess so," Pete said in a low voice.

"What?"

"Yes I know him," Pete answered. "Is he alright?" About that time a little dog popped up in Pete's arms. "What the heck!"

"There you are you my little sugar bugger," said Lou. "Ok, we are all here. Let's go home Pete." Behind Lou an ambulance had just arrived and apparently it was there to get Lou.

The policeman looked at Pete. "I understand that you do know him but we have to take him to the hospital just to make sure he's alright. Regardless if he was the one jumping in front of the car or not, he has to be checked out, that's the law."

"Jumping out in front of cars?" Pete said with a puzzled look on his face. "He was jumping into the traffic in hopes to get hit, for money? Are you kidding me? Damn it Lou!" Pete looked down at the man he had once Idolized his whole life.

"Yes sir, that's old leaping Lou alright. He must be really down on his luck this time. He's getting too old to keep doing this kind of stuff. He's going to wind up getting really hurt or killed. If I was a close friend, I would see about getting him some real help and a place, nice place to stay, I'm just saying." With that the policeman walked off.

Pete turned and walked over to Lou lying inside the ambulance. "Hey there Pete, you got Buster? He's the best one out of all my Busters."

"Damn Lou, you're crazy. That officer just told me you've been jumping into traffic on purpose. Really!" shouted Pete. "You try to get their insurance money or something? What the hell has happened to you?"

The ambulance driver came around the corner of the truck. "Sir, sorry, we have to go." The door to the vehicle shut in front of Pete. Lou didn't have a chance to say a word and the rescue team drove off.

Pete felt something warm licking his hands and he looked down to realize he was still holding Lou's dog, Buster. "Ain't this starting out to be just a lovely day?" Pete said to the dog as he looked up to the sky, as if toward heaven and the rain kept pouring down.

Chapter 31

A Little Off the Top

IT WAS A WARM SUMMER DAY as Dud walked into the Carolina Barber Shop. The bell rang as the door opened and closed. The place was full of the sounds of electric clippers and customers' conversations going full blast. But they all got real quiet when they saw who just walked in the door. You could still hear the rhythm and popping sound of Old Rufus's shoe shine cloth working away… wap, wap, wap, pop, pop, pop, wap. His back was facing the door so he could not see Dud. He was hard at it, making a mirror finish on his customer's tan Johnson Murphy's at his shoe shine station on the back wall of the store. Saturday morning was a busy time for the most popular barber shop in town. The Ernest Koken hydraulic barber chairs were full of customers getting cleaned up and ready to go out on the town for a Saturday night date or just in to get their every other weekly hair cut to look good for the next workweek. Dud looked around the room tipping his hat to the onlookers and took his place for his haircut. It didn't take long for the noise level to rise again.

Folks would find their seat in front of their favorite barber or just stand beside the many coat racks if there was no room to sit. The Carolina Barber Shop was a classic barber shop, elongated in length with ten stations, small black and white tile dotted the floor, worn out leather benches and chairs lined the wall on the left, with the coat and hat rack about every twenty feet. The cash register was in the middle of the store between the barbers. The shoe shine station in the back could accommodate six men at one time. Behind the barbers was a huge mirror that ran the full length of the room. And full of the best barbers in town, this was the place to be for both haircuts and great conversations. If you wanted to know about things going on in town this was where you needed to be. Regardless of how busy the barber shop was, sitting or standing, they all were waiting for their turn to get their ears lowered. By the time Dud walked in Lloyd had just gotten through with his last client and saw Dud take his sit to wait. Lloyd had the first chair in the shop. That meant he had seniority and that he had worked his way up to the front of the rest. He was the one everyone wanted. But still, everyone had their own favorite. The whole shop was abuzz with the news of Pete getting arrested and on top of that, here comes the Chief of Police himself to get a haircut.

"Next," shouted Lloyd as he cleaned off the chair from the last patron. No one moved. They all knew Dud was not only the Chief of Police but he was Lloyd's brother as well. So they all knew to wait a little longer, knowing Lloyd would be worth the wait.

"Well then, if nobody else is ready, it looks like you're next Dud. Have a seat and take a load off," said Lloyd. As he pumped the hydraulic barber chair up and down to get the height for Dud just right Lloyd asked, "Alright brother what should it be, how you like it?" As if Lloyd hadn't cut Dub's hair a thousand times, plus with the thick wiry hair Lloyd would put a number two guard on his chippers and cut that old thick stuff off anyway. Pretty easy cut to say the least.

"Just a little off the top. You know Lloyd, clean it up a little. You know the drill. I have a meeting with the Mayor this afternoon."

"I've got it brother, a haircut that doesn't look like a new haircut. Will do," Lloyd said as he placed the cape over Dud and wrapped a small strip of paper around his neck. He then secured the cape around his neck with a metal chip. "No way is any hair getting down that shirt," Lloyd thought.

" Hey Bill, did you hear the one where these two old boys are setting on the front porch?" said Red Mitchell sitting in the chair beside of Dud and talking loud enough so all could hear the new joke of the week.

"No, I don't think I have," said Bill Patella, the owner of Carolina Barber Shop. "Tell it brother."

"Yea these two old country boys and their dog were on the front porch and the old blue tick hound was laying there between the two men, licking itself down there in his privates."

"You don't say."

"Yea and one ole boy looks over at the other fella, then looks down at the dog and says, 'I wish I could do that'. A couple of seconds go by and the other fella looks at his buddy, then looks down at the dog and says, yeah, but the that old dog will bite you."

"Yeah but that dog will bite you, I heard that," said Lloyd, like that was the first time he had ever heard that old worn-out joke, as he and the rest of the barber shop broke out in laughter.

"Yeah that's a good one Red. That old dog will bite you," said Bill as he was finishing his cut and was ready for the next patron. "Please tell Mabel I said hello when you get home Red."

"Sure will. Bill, Lloyd, Dud you boys take care of yourself."

"Will do Red," the three said in unison.

Lloyd leaned over and whispered in Dub's ear at the same time pumping the handle on the barber chair. "You know everyone will be listening to what you say." Dud turned his head away from Lloyd, as if he didn't hear a word. Lloyd turned the chair around so he could see everyone looking at him and Dud and started on his hair cut.

"Sure is hot out there ain't it?"

"Sure is."

"How's Mom?"

"She's good. I talked to her yesterday, but she sure misses dad."

"Don't we all," said Lloyd. "I heard her sister's boy got his picture in the paper."

"He sure did, but you didn't have to bring that up, did you Lloyd?" Dud said in a loud voice.

The room was listening to every word the two brothers were saying. Then someone in the chair a couple of chairs down spoke up. "Why did you go and arrest the town's hero, Chief? That boy's a good boy and a war vet. Your men should be ashamed, hauling that poor boy in like that."

Dud turned so fast in the chair he was lucky Lloyd didn't cut his ear off. "Look here," said Dud. "First of all that good old boy broke the law by striking a police officer and starting a riot. Now that's what got him in jail in the first place," Dud shouted to the group of onlookers.

"Everyone knows that Johnny Law started it," said a customer.

"Yea, he's a hot head Chief. He's the one that needed to be arrested," said someone in the crowd.

"No, don't arrest Johnny Law, not Johnny, the one that started it. Let's arrest Pete," said Rufus the shoe shine man. "Go talk to Pete Hall, the owner of the place. He'll tell you."

"He's damn lucky he got off without seeing the insides of a court room," said Dud.

Bill Patella turned his customer's chair around, trying to cut off the conversation before this thing got completely out of control. The whole barber shop wanted to be in the conversation and it was so obvious they cared about Pete. Lloyd, too, turned Dud's chair around to defuse the situation himself.

"Thanks for opening the can of worms big brother."

"You knew we had to say something about it Dud. Everybody in town has been talking about it for days."

"Hey Chief, hope you got plans for a different line of work come November."

"You people," said Dud shaking his head in disgust.

"Hey Tommy, how about some music? Turn on the radio or something," said Lloyd. Tommy was the barber down the line closest to the radio. As the sound of Dean Martin's song, *Its Amore*, floated through the shop Lloyd sensed the situation was losing its steam.

"I knew not to come in here," said Dud under his breath.

"It's good that you did brother. It's going to be ok," said Lloyd as he was about to apply the hot shaving cream to his brother's neck and ears to finish off the hair cut.

"Are you finished?" asked Dud, as he quickly studied on how to get off the hook and leave this barber shop full of rude townspeople before he really said something he would regret.

"I sure am," said Lloyd, as he wiped the hot shaving cream off his hands with a towel before he tried to shaved him and removed the barber's cape that had collected little if any of Dud's hair that was cut. "Next," shouted Lloyd, and with that Dud stepped down from the chair and got his hat off the coat rack, wiping some hair off the front of his shirt. He then glared at the towns people in a defiant way as he adjusted his gun belt. No one said a word while Dud stared, looking down the line at each customer sitting in their barber chair, looking as if he was coming to shoot them down or something.

"You people," said Dud shaking his head as he paid Lloyd his dollar for a twenty five cent haircut. He then turned and was happy to exit on his way out the door as the bell rang.

In a few minutes the shop was back to normal with talk of next year's high school football team, pretty girls and dirty jokes, just regular barber shop stuff. Everyone loved Pete. He was a hero to a lot of boxing fans.

And in the hearts of most folks in the barber shop and in town they knew Chief Dud was just dead wrong, and the elections coming up in the fall would prove it.

Chapter32

Recovering

"BEFORE YOU SEE YOUR SON I want you two to know that the improvement and recovery from the brain trauma will be very slow. Years, not months, but there is some good news regarding the leg," said Doctor Ben Kilmon, Chief Sergeant of Walter Reed Army Hospital. "There was enough bone structure left to support his new prophesies. And the carotid artery was not traumatized from the blast." But the painful truth, the Doctor went on to say, "it will take months, if not years, before Pete will walk without his crutches. Plus the painful sores and bruises will always be there, along with the battle fatigue and sleepless nights of reoccurring nightmares. In all, Pete's new civilian lifestyle would be hard to adapt to under regular circumstances much less being a paraplegic." In 1945 they did not have the technology to build an artificial leg good enough to stop the painful sores and bruising that would occur.

Jim and Knobby Smith sat there dumbfounded in that big old office on the top floor of the hospital listening to the Doctor's grim diagnosis of Pete's catastrophic injuries. They had received word from family members and friends on the horrible conditions of Walter Reed so Jim and Knobby were there to retrieve their beloved son. They both nervously looked around the room as the physician rattled on with his sophisticated rhetoric that neither of them wanted to hear or talk about. They wanted their son and that's all. Suddenly Knobby stood up and motioned to Jim to do the same. She extended her right hand. "I thank you for all you and your staff has done Sir. Now it's time for us to take our son home and let the good Lord and our families' love start healing our boy. A hospital is no place for the soul to heal."

"You are so right Mrs. Smith," said Doctor Kilmon. "I think he will be able to travel in a couple of weeks."

"Good, we'll be ready first thing tomorrow morning."

"No Mrs. Smith, I said two weeks," repeated the Doctor for the second time.

Knobby was a pretty good sized girl and she used that size to intimidate him as she walked right up to the Doctor's face. "Look here Doctor, from all that I have seen up here so far, you boys are covered up with broken bodies. And if that son of ours is strong enough to withstand this hospital, with the lack of care and incompetence I've seen around here, much less a bomb blast or two, I think a seven hour car ride would be downright therapeutic." Jim walked closer to Knobby as if he was saying back down old girl.

The Doctor realized she was correct in her observation. He then gave in by saying, "Yes Mrs. Smith, you're right. I was just looking out for what I thought was best for the boy and I do understand and appreciate your position as a parent. I will have his discharge papers ready tomorrow morning, first thing. You are truly a strong family and I'm sure

Pete will be just fine in your care."

"All right then, I'm going to see my son. Where is he?" Knobby asked, knowing she had won the battle.

"We'll have to get his paper work in order first before you can see him," said the Doctor. "Again we'll see you tomorrow."

"No, I want to see him now, now is good. We have been waiting two years and I am not leaving today till I see Pete. Don't you worry your big brain anymore on us, we'll find him ourselves!"

And with that the Smiths left the Doctor's office and marched their way down the hall to the first elevator in search of Pete's room. Floor to floor and hall after hall they walked down asking everyone they met where could they find their son Pete. Hall after hallway and about an hour and several elevators, six escalators and a dozen more hallways, they arrived at the ward where Pete was located. Pete's name was on the board outside the amputee's ward but there was no one at the nurses' station, and no nurses in the ward for that matter. So they slowly walked up and down the rows of beds in search of Pete. Jim looked over and saw Pete's name on the footboard of his bed.

"Knobby over here," he called.

They finally found him; Pete was curled up in a ball in the bed. From the looks and smell of him, he had not shaved or washed in days. The bed pan was full and the bed sheets were filthy. The whole ward was overcrowded with beds of dirty soldiers. Knobby stared, with tears starting to form, as she noticed the entire hospital wing was in a state of disrepair. It was horrible.

"Who in the world is in charge here?" Knobby hollered out for some attention. A surprised orderly looked up as he walked into the ward and saw the two civilians. He quickly backed out of the ward and ran down the hall, after seeing the look on Knobby and Jim's faces.

"Hey where the heck you are going?" Big Jim said, trying to reach out to grab the young man by the arm.

Knobby looked back at Pete. "Son, its Mother. Are you ok? Pete Smith I'm talking to you, answer your Mother," said Knobby, as she reached over and touched his forehead. Knobby could not believe what she was seeing in this hospital. Pete finally opened his eyes and saw the sight of his family. He thought he was still dreaming. This was something he had been wishing for months. "Pete can you hear me son?" Knobby inquired again.

With a tear rolling down his face, Pete looked up at his Mother and said, "Yes Mam , please get me home, please take me home Mother."

Jim grabbed his son's hand and tearfully said, "Don't you worry boy, it's time to go."

The reunion was interrupted by a young nurse standing in the doorway with both hands on her hips and a scowl on her face.

"What in the heck is going on in here? Who give you permission to be here? You two are not suppose to be in here at all," said Nurse Wanda Brown as she entered the ward.

"Well that's pretty obvious from the looks and condition of this room and these men," said Knobby.

"You don't have any rights to be here. You need to get out now," the nurse ordered once again.

"It's Wanda, the wicked witch of the west," one patient cried out.

Jim spoke up. "Our son gives us all the right I need. Don't you worry your pretty little head over us; we're getting the hell out of here as soon as we get our boy dressed."

The nurse looked over to the orderly. "Call the MP's. They will take care of this situation." The other soldiers in their beds were getting in the action by making all kinds of noise, beating the bed pans and shouting. The whole hospital was in a buzz with all that was going on in that ward. Nurse Brown was fit to be tied.

At that moment the door opened, and in walked Lieutenant Major, Mildred Wilkes.

"Attention on deck," someone shouted and with that, all the wild noise and commotion came to a halt. Nurse Brown turned and saw her as attention was called.

"Yes, can I help you Lieutenant Major?" said Nurse Brown as she walked up to the officer.

"Yes, you surly can young lady. I would like to inform you that you have been relieved of your duties, right here and now, nurse." Millie walked right up to her face close enough to bite her.

"What? You can't tell me anything like that. I work for General Robert B. Simpson."

"Well that's fine, but you'll find that General Simpson is no longer in charge of you or anyone else in this hospital. I have taken over this area and you are in my ward now. You are no longer needed. You need to see the Personal Officer on your way out."

"You can't do this. I have my rights! What is this all about? I haven't done anything wrong."

"They will have your transfer papers ready in a couple of days."

"What, you can't, you have no right. You..." The nurse was speechless. She seemed to wilt under the Lieutenant Major's presence.

"Yes I can, and yes, I just did," the Lieutenant Major said, and then she turned to Pete's bed, and kneeled at his side. The whole ward went nuts as the soldiers started shouting, howling and calling nurse Brown names. She picked up her things and walked out of the ward and down the hall, mad and humiliated.

Pete looked up at the Lieutenant. "Damn it Millie, where the hell have you been? This place is a hell hole."

Millie reached for his hand. "I'm so sorry Pete. We'll straighten this place up in a few days, and I'm here now," she said as the two hugged and kissed.

He looked over at Jim and Knobby. "Hey Mom and Dad, this is Millie. She's my girl," he said and they kissed again.

Jim and Knobby looked at each other. "Damn Knobby, that boy of yours sure knows how to pick'em," said Jim with a laugh. The two stood there with tears streaming down their faces knowing their boy was in good hands at last. Pete would soon be leaving Walter Reed for the VA hospital in Durham North Carolina and it just happened to be the same hospital Millie was transferring to as well. They would never be apart again.

Chapter 33

Reunion

PETE COULD NOT HELP THE feeling he was having ever since he arrived at the hospital. All those years as a patient was rushing back in his mind. It all started at the field hospital in Italy, then the Royal Sussex hospital in Brighton England, then state side to Walter Reed in Washington DC, which seemed like forever. The ride didn't stop there. He was almost home when he arrived at the nearby VA hospital in Durham. For years it was countless trips back and forth to the Alamance County hospital and years at the Kernodle Clinic. But the good news about this trip, he was a visitor, not a patient, he thought as the elevator door opened to the third floor of the Charlotte Regional Hospital.

"Now aren't you a sight for sore eyes," said Lou as Pete walked into his room. Lou was wearing a straight jacket of some kind, and his hands were restrained and tied to the bed. He was not going anywhere, Pete thought.

"Here, Millie got you some flowers." Pete laid them on a table.

"Thanks, they look delicious, you guys shouldn't have."

"Delicious," said Pete.

"Yea didn't you hear, I'm crazy, I might eat the damn things or something like that? Who knows?" Lou laughed with a twinkle in his eyes.

"She got them...you know how women are," Pete said as he looked around the room. He had a look of something on his mind. "How you feeling, better?"

"I guess so. I still don't understand why I am here all tied up and all. It's not like I got anywhere to go."

"Jump out in front of any cars lately?" asked Pete.

"Hell I was just trying to get a little spending money."

"That's not what the police and the insurance companies were saying."

"I wasn't trying to sue the insurance companies. Hell I'm small time; I try to stay under the radar."

"Small time Lou," said Pete.

"That's right," shouted Lou as he tried to pull out of the restraints on his arms and legs. "That's me, nothing big, a dollar here and there, that's all Pete. Honest."

"Ok Lou, calm down, I understand."

"How 'bout this jacket? I ain't no animal!"

"I'll see about that too, Uncle Lou," said Pete, noticing that someone was at the door.

"Hey there Lou, remember me, it's Sleepy Johnson." Sleepy made his way into the room and he, too, brought flowers.

"Yea, I remember your short, smart ass. What the hell are you doing here? Want to wear my jacket asshole?" said Lou.

"Now Lou, Sleepy was just being nice coming up here. You take it easy on him. He's from back home and an old friend of yours to boot," said Pete.

"Oh hell, I was just messing with you, Stumpy."

"That's Sleepy, not Stumpy."

"Ok, you two ease up. I feel like I'm back in the ring around you two," Pete said as he found a vase to put all the flowers in.

"By the way, where the hell is Buster, my dog?" asked Lou.

"He was shitting all over the gym floor last time I saw him," said Sleepy with a laugh.

Lou turned to Sleepy. "Great, Pete's taken you in too," said Lou.

"No, I work there old man. Remember I'm a corner man and a pretty good one I must say."

"You'd be the only one that would," said Lou with a laugh.

"Damn, you two are like a couple of old wash women," said Pete. "Now look Lou, we are going to try to get you out of here but you have to promise me you are going to act right. I can't have you acting crazy and jumping in front of cars and stuff. Can I have you word? Your word was always good to me."

Lou looked up at a Pete with all sincerity. "You got my word son; I need your help Pete. Please help me." Lou's look of desperation said it all.

"Ok then," said Pete as he touched Lou on the arm.

"What the hell Pete! Are you going to bring that crazy old man to live with us at the gym? You must be the one that's crazy," said Sleepy.

Both Lou and Pete looked at each and then they both shouted at the same time, "Shut up Sleepy!"

Chapter 34

The Real Deal

"I'M TELLING YOU GUYS HE IS the real deal. Wait till ya'll see this guy," said Sleepy chewing on his cigar, as Lou and Pete made their way down from the front office to ring side in the old gym. They watched as Tony and Larry were helping, "loud mouth" Randy up to his feet and was fixing his head piece that was turned all the way around facing the wrong way. Randy's father, Randy Senior, fought for Lou years ago, or actually he just worked out in the gym. Randy Senior was never very good. And just like his son, Randy Senior always tried to give Pete a hard time. It was Senior who got beat-up by Pete when Pete first started to work here with Lou. Like father and son, these two had the same disposition.

"Let go of me," said Randy as he pulled away from the two guys helping. "I'm ok. That was a lucky punch. I'll get him next round." Then before anyone could stop him, he fell back to the canvas flat on his face with the head piece still on backwards.

"You are as big of an ass as your dad was," said Sleepy. "The next round my ass! He knocked you out three times. How about you guys get him out of here and let Doc take a look at him," Sleepy told the two boys helping Randy out of the ring.

"What happened to 'loud mouth'?" asked Pete.

"He got his clock rung, that's what happened sir," said Nelson. "That's my brother Al who just took your boy out of here."

Nelson and Albert Flynn were Irish brothers from Boston by way of the U.S. Army and were both stationed in Fort Bragg when they were discharged. That's how they got to the Carolina's. They were both good fighters in their own right, but Al was a little special. He was bigger, a heavy weight and a true south paw. And they both were looking for a gym to call home and needing a trainer and promoter like Pete and Lou. And of course everyone knew Pete and Lou were the best in the Charlotte area, if not the south.

"This kid is a hard hitting machine with a left arm like a cannon," said Sleepy with excitement.

"Lefty, really?" Pete asked. "How did you boys get in here? Who sent you to me?"

"He did," the two brothers both answered as they pointed at Lou. Lou just looked curious as if they were crazy or had confused his identity with someone else.

"Lou, what the hell. Lou, how and where did you find such talent?"

Lou turned around in a defiant tone and spoke up to Pete. "Now wait a minute Pete. Sleepy is right. These boys are good. And this gym needs some new blood. Hell, when was the last time we had a contender around here? For months these two tried to get time in your ring to show what they had and finally they got a chance to show off their talents. You got not one, but two diamonds in the rough here and I say we keep them," said Lou.

Pete walked over to the two boys and shook their hands. "Looks like I don't have a choice," said Pete. "Welcome to your new gym. We start training first thing in the morning. Get your gear and Sleepy will show you your lockers and where you put your stuff."

"Thank you Mister Smith," said Albert. " We won't let you down I promise," and with that they both started shaking their heads in agreement.

"Ok boys we'll see you later." Pete looked over at Lou once again and waited till the brothers left the gym with Sleepy. As soon as the door shut Pete turned to Lou. "Lou what is going on here? You don't just find talent like that walking off the streets, not in Charlotte, North Carolina anyway. Where the hell did they come from," ordered Pete.

Lou knew he was caught and there was nothing to do but tell him the truth. "Tom," said Lou. "If you needed to know, they're his family."

"Not Tom O'Leary, the damn mobster that ran you out of town years ago? That damn Tom? I guess Blinky Palermo is their grandfather!" shouted Pete.

"No you don't understand, wait Pete," said Lou.

"Wait for what? A bullet if he doesn't get his money this time? Hell, it took me years to pay off the S.O.B. the last time, and there damn sure ain't going to be a next time Lou, I mean it." Pete turned his back to Lou as he walked over to the ring and stared at nothing.

"Hold on Pete, calm down, it's not like that at all," said Lou. "These boys don't know about Tommy and me, plus this whole thing was all Tom's doing. He's their Uncle, plus he is dying of cancer. He wants the boys to have a chance of a good life, not like him, a mobster, but someone people can look up to, someone like you maybe."

Pete then turned back around to face Lou. "O shut the hell up Lou. Don't you try to sweet talk me. I know what you're doing. You're always working an angle aren't you? And there's only one thing and one thing only, that motivates you, money. Now how much is he paying us?"

"Us," said Lou. "I knew you would go along with it."

"You damn right it's us! There ain't no way you are doing this out of the love you and Tom have for each other. So if I'm in this mess, what's the story?"

"Ok, you see Tom wants us to train and promote the two boys so no one will know Tom is involved with their careers. Plus here's the good part. He will pay us to train them."

"Tom is going to pay us to train his nephews?"

"That's right," said Lou, "and he only wants half of the prize money."

Pete's face turned pale, as if all the blood had run out of it. "Half! Half my ass! You tell that son of a bitch, he can bet on them just like anyone else does and that's all. Half, I'm not paying him one dime. You understand me old man," shouted Pete.

Pete had never been so mad in his life. It took all he could do not to hit Lou. Lou knew it and was feeling right ashamed of the situation. Lou stood there without saying a word. Pete turned as he was walking away and looked at Lou once more. "You tell him thanks, but we don't need his money," said Pete. He then stopped, and looked Lou right in the eye. "I lost you one time because of Old Tom's tricks. I can't go through that again, I need you here Lou. Plus those boys are already good. They won't need much training anyway. It will be alright." With that Pete walked back to his office.

Lou knew Pete was right. Getting involved with Tommy again would be Lou's downfall, just like the last time. Lou started to feel another coughing spell coming on so he pulled out his handkerchief. He was right and started coughing a little bit. "I sure am coughing a lot here lately," he thought as he looked at the handkerchief and saw the blood. It was a little more than the last time. He wiped his mouth and thought nothing more of it. He turned and walked off to the locker room to clean up.

"We are going to have a real contender," he thought to himself as he walked away.

Chapter 35

The Cow Palace

PETE'S DREAM WAS COMING true. The gym was at full occupancy. The place was packed nonstop with reporters, boxing people and fans. It was great times for the fight business, and as for Lou, Sleepy and Pete, it had never been better. The brothers Flynn had given this place the shot in the arm that they all needed. But Pete, being Pete and forever the cautious one, was always waiting for the next shoe to drop, but it never did. Money was coming in and all was right with the world.

"Hey Pete, phone call," Loud Mouth shouted out.

"Tell them I'm busy and call back later," he said as he was working on an old headgear chin strap for someone.

"No I think you ought to get this one. The fellow's name is Hayward Jones."

"*The* Hayward Jones," Pete replied, "Amos Lincoln's manager?"

"That's the one, Amos "Big Train" Lincoln's manager. He would like to talk to you now," shouted Randy.

"Ok Loud Mouth I'm coming," said Pete, as he grabbed for his crutches and put away the stuff he had been working on.

"Hey Pete, Hayward Jones here," said the man on the other end of the telephone. "Looks like you boys got a real contender over there in Charlotte."

"Yea, we're pretty proud of Al and how he's coming along, six straight wins all by knockout, yes sir we are," said Pete.

"Well how would you boys like to come out to California and take a crack at my fellow, 'Big Train'?" said Hayward. "We're lined up to fight Eddie Machen for next year and your boy has a lot of his same mannerisms, but Machen likes to fight at the Cow Palace in San Francisco."

"Well to be honest with you Hayward, we don't have the money to go all the way to San Francisco to spar with your boy," said Pete.

"No, no, I'm not talking about sparing at all. It would be the real deal, your boy and mine, but here in Texas, not at the Cow Palace. What you say to that Pete?"

"I don't know if he is ready for all that."

"I'll make sure the money is right."

"Yea…. I still don't know Hayward," said Pete again.

"Plus, pay all your travel expenses to boot," said Hayward.

"We'll see," said Pete. " We are still having negotiations with Cleveland Williams' people. We'll see. I'll call you back in a couple of days." Pete hung up the phone, knowing full well the "Big Cat" Williams' people had not called.

"Big Cat Williams' people called too," said Randy. Wait till I tell the brothers. They'll go crazy with this news!"

"News hell! You're not going to tell a soul anything that you heard here, you got me?" Pete walked closer to Randy. "You understand me?"

"Yes sir, I do," replied Randy as he looked down at the floor.

"Now shut your loud mouth, and go get Lou," said Pete, as he sat pondering over the call that just took place. Amos "Big Train" Lincoln, damn we have arrived. Before you know it Ernie Terrell's folks will be calling, thought Pete. Whoever called, Pete was ready to field the phone call.

Lou was sitting on his bed wiping the blood that was running down from his nose again. The problem these last couple of months had gotten worse and still he had not told a soul. He looked up as he heard the knock on the door.

"Yea Lou, Pete wants to see you. It's important," said Randy.

"Hold on Loud Mouth. I'm coming, I'm coming," said Lou, as he quickly tried to clean up both the room and himself.

Randy opened the door on Lou and saw all the blood on Lou's face, plus the bed spread and napkins and toilet paper in little balls on the floor at his feet. "Damn Lou, is you hurt, did someone cut you?" shouted Randy as he rushed over to Lou's side to see what was wrong with him.

"No, get your damn hands off me you fool. I'm just fine," said Lou as he pushed Randy off.

"Fine hell, you're bleeding like a stuck hog, old man," said Randy as he rose up and looked down at Lou.

"Look boy it's just a nose bleed. Trust me I'm ok Randy, and what's so damn important you had to bust in and tell me?"

"Pete just got off the phone with Hayward Jones. He's ..." Lou stopped him.

"I know who he is Randy. What did he say?" asked Lou.

"Well he wants to...no I ain't going to tell you. Pete told me not to tell anyone that Big Train wants to fight Al at the Cow Palace, I think."

"Ok Loud Mouth you kept your secret. I'll just have to ask Pete for myself. You run along and I'll be there directly. Let me get myself together. Tell Pete I'm coming."

"Will do Lou, you take your time," said Randy as he ran off to tell Pete about Lou.

"Well, those two secrets are out of the bag. Hell Loud Mouth will have it on the six o'clock news that we are fighting Big Train, and that I'm dying," said Lou to himself as he got off the bed and headed down the hall to see Pete. "We're headed to the Cow Palace. I bet it's Houston Texas? Damn ain't that something!" said Lou as he got close enough to Pete so he could hear.

"Where the hell did you hear…, oh never mind," said Pete after realizing he sent Randy to fetch him. "No I don't think so, I'm thinking more like Cleveland Williams."

"Big Cat" shouted Lou. "That boy of ours ain't got a chance with Big Cat. He will eat him alive," said Lou rubbing his head.

"Well who else should it be, Zory Folley, Bob Foster, Jerry Quarry, Thad Spencer, George "Scrap Iron" Johnson? You name the fighter Lou." Pete stopped talking for a second and looked closer at Lou. "Is that blood on your shirt?" said Pete as he walked up to Lou to check it out. "Damn Lou, are you ok?"

"I'm fine. Eddie Machen, that's who we'll fight, no, no, even better, Ernie Terrell."

"Ernie Terrell!" shouted Pete. "Are you crazy, that's six foot six inches of Ernie Terrell. We would have to train Al using a ladder!"

"Yea, but he's only about two hundred pounds and our boy Al can get in close and stay right in his ribs all night till Ernie drops like a lead balloon."

"The question is how we are going to get Terrell's people to agree to that fight?" asked Pete.

"Don't you worry about that old boy, I have that handled," said Lou. "You just get our fighter ready. I'm still the promoter around here."

"Yes sir, you sure are Uncle Lou, you surly are," said Pete and with that the two walked out of the gym together.

"We going somewhere to fight somebody, I'll tell you that!" shouted Lou on his way out the door.

Chapter 36

Out of the Crowd

"FIFTEEN MINUTES BEFORE THE FIGHT is all the time we have," Sleepy said.

"Fifteen minutes, that's all?" said Lou, as he was pacing up and down the hall inside the Madison Square Garden. "Fifteen minutes? You've got to be kidding me. How the hell does this kind of thing happen?" said Lou rubbing his head.

"All I know is that we were standing in line with a ticket in our hand waiting to go in and see the fights, when some guy came up and asked if Al was a fellow named Charlie Green, the fight professional. Al said, maybe who wants to know? He didn't say a word, stood there, sized him up and figured he was the right weight class and said 'ok, get ready, you have about fifteen minutes,' so here we are," said Sleepy.

"Does Al know that he's about to fight *the* Jose Torres, and that he is taking Jimmy Ralston's, from Buffalo, place in this fight? Jimmy Ralston and Jose Torres… are you kidding me!" said Lou.

"I don't think he knows much about anything, other than he was picked out of a crowd to fight the former light heavyweight champion of the world, and he is so excited Lou," said Sleepy.

"Ok, here's the deal, win lose or draw we can't tell Pete. Pete cannot hear a word of this fight, do you understand me Sleepy? We were suppose to show Al the big time fight game in New York, not put him in it, and who the hell is Charlie Green?" said Lou, still rubbing his head.

"I understand Lou, but this is a big fight. You know Pete is going to find out. Hell, he might be hearing it on the radio back home. I sure wish Pete was here. He would know what to do."

"Don't you worry; I've been in this fight game longer than Pete. Now let's go in there and be calm, cool, and collected, and get our boy ready to fight, damn it! That's what we are going to do," said Lou.

As they opened the door to the locker room Al was sitting on the table with his shorts hanging off his shoes. "What the hell is this Al?" bellowed Lou.

"They don't fit… the shorts, I can't wear them. They're too big."

"O' hell that's ok, we'll get some tape or string or something and get you fixed up," said Sleepy.

"Yea, that's no big deal, but this fight sure can be. You know that, right?" Lou emphasized.

"Yes sir, it was like God picked me out from everybody," said Al with excitement in his voice.

"No son that was a fight promoter praying that he was not going to lose his ass because the other fighter was a no show, that's what this was! Now you do understand you do not have to fight this guy?" said Lou.

"Look Lou," said Al. "I understand its one in a million chance for me and I feel now is the time, right now. So let's get me taped up, get my shorts to fit, and tell me how great a boxer I am and get me ready. I have a fight to win!"

"That's all I needed to hear," said Lou. "Sleepy go get some tape and some string. Our boy is fighting in about ten minutes."

As they entered the Garden Al could not believe the pure size of it all. The crowd was mostly pulling for Torres and the only fans Al had was his corner man Sleepy, and his manager, Lou. In Al's mind they were the only ones that mattered anyway.

As the ring of the bell sounded the fight began. The two started feeling each other out with a couple of jabs apiece for the first few seconds. Then with a string of hard hitting punches Al went straight to work. He hit Torres with a couple of right crosses and a hard left hook that shocked Torres and the crowd reacted with cheers, realizing that this up and coming newcomer was giving the former champ all he wanted. Torres looked like an old man at the age of 33. He had not fought since April of sixty -eight and it showed. Al kept the pressure on with hard hitting jabs and hooks. And out of nowhere to everyone's surprise, Al landed a hard and powerful right cross that sent Torres down to the canvas. The crowd was in shock and Al seemed to have won over some of the fans as they began to cheer for Al.

"That 'a boy," shouted Lou. "Holy shit, now get your ass over here in the corner!"

Referee Johnny LoBianco started his count as the crowd and Al, were stunned in disbelief at what they just saw. The former champion made it to his feet on the count of eight and the fight started again. The crowd was into it now shouting Al's name; the Garden had a fight on its hands and it was truly handpicked. Al was looking great, giving shot after shot to Torres. To Torres' credit he could still take a punch and Al was putting them on him, left cross, right jab, jab, and a hard left to Torres' jaw. Torres was on complete defense and counting down the seconds for the bell to ring and it finally did.

As Al rushed back to his corner with a bounce is his step and feeling pretty good on the first round, Lou and Sleepy were on the ready. "My God kid, you look great out there," said Lou.

"Thanks Lou, he ain't all that," said Al, still excited about what just happened.

"Now listen to me," Lou directed Al's attention. "Be careful. He's hurt; you hurt him pretty good so watch out. An old fighter will use all kinds of tricks to win. Just keep your eyes open for rabbit or low punches, you understand me?"

"Yes sir I do," was his reply.

"Keep it up Al," said Sleepy "and watch out for the rabbit punches in the back of your head. He's known for those."

Al shook his head yes to them both, replaced his mouth piece and waited for the second round to start. The bell rang and once again it quickly was going Al's way. Al kept throwing hard hitting punches of all kinds; jabs, upper cuts, crosses, hooks. Al was having his way with the former champ and once again Al unloaded a thunderous right hook that floored Torres for the second time. The crowd was now at a fever pitch and the world was watching a new rising star in Albert Flynn. The referee started his count, but the bell rang and saved Torres from defeat. Torres was then helped back to his corner by his handlers, as they worked on saving their fighter's outcome.

Lou jumped off his feet shouting, "You can't do that! That's a violation!" Lou kept shouting at the referee. "He has to go under his own power to the corner ref."   Lou argued to no avail.

The state law at the time was a boxer who is knocked down cannot be saved by the bell till the end of the fight, not the round, and cannot receive any assistance. He has to go back to the corner under his own power.

"Ok, Al you are still doing great. Just watch that son of a bitch; looks like the house wants him to win. Well you can change all of that. Just keep it up, just go after him," said Lou.

Sleepy didn't say a word. He could not believe this was happening. 'We have a real contender. This kid has what it takes,' Sleepy thought.

Torres knew he had to do something to stop this kid's attempt of ending his career. After all, he was once the champion of the world, and repeating that chance again was all Torres was studying on, despite the effects Al was showcasing tonight.

 The bell sounded and the round started, and once again Al was all over Torres. He hit him with a couple of strong jabs but nothing like the ones before and Torres went down again. This time was different however. Torres just seemed to go down without much of a fight. He went down on one knee and the ref came in for a standing eight count. Torres seemed to be resting and catching his breath. All the while Al was standing there with his back turned away from Torres. He did not realize what Torres was doing so he started going back to his corner, totally unaware of Torres' strategy. As a result, after the so called standing eight count, Torres sprung to his feet and caught Al completely unaware and flat footed. By the time Al realized what was happening Torres had already thrown the haymaker that caught Al right in the back of the head. He was floored by a sucker punch from behind out of nowhere.

"What the hell," yelled Lou as he jumped to his feet and shouted foul, but there was no need. It was all over. In ten seconds Jose Torres threw his arms in the air in a victory sign. But everyone in the Garden knew his career was over. The boo's started and they would not stop till he left the area. Lou and Sleepy ran over to their boy. His arm was hanging over the bottom rope. The rest of his body was laid out like he had been run over by a train.

"Quick, turn him over on his back," said Lou, as Sleepy and Lou turned him over to check on his breathing.

"Is he alive, is he ok?" said Sleepy.

"Yea, he's ok. Hey talk to me Al," said Lou as he broke open the smelling salts.

Torres started to walk over and say something but Lou stopped him. "Hey! Get the hell out of here you sucker punching son of a bitch!" yelled Lou.

"That was pretty shitty," said Sleepy as he was helping Al back to his seat on the stool in the corner.

Torres turned, with his head hanging low, and stepped out of the ring, knowing the fight and his career was over.

He did have a few more fights before his career finished, but he was never the same boxer. His career was truly ended by a kid that was picked out of a crowd.

The three sat on the train headed back home in silence until Sleepy spoke up. "Well that was a hell of a trip to the Big Apple!"

"Don't you worry Kid," said Lou. "This is not going to end your career. You were robbed by that cheating ass hole."

"I'm not worried Lou. Besides, I didn't use my real name," said Al.

"What?"

"No, I told them my name was Green, Charley Green. They didn't ask for any I.D. and the guy in the crowd thought I was some fellow named Green, so I said sure, you can call me Charley Green ".

"Well I'll be," said Lou grinning from ear to ear.

"You are picking up on this fight game pretty fast," said Sleepy and they all three laughed as they headed home.

Chapter 37

Nightmares and Liquor Sells

PETE CRAWLED ON THE GROUND like a snake, laying in the mud and dirt, making sure he kept low enough and trying his best to get away from the machine gun fire. He then turned and looked in horror upon the faces of his dead Army buddies, their bodies stacked in a pile like cord wood. The image of their dead, lifeless bodies was haunting. He then turned to go down a cornrow, to escape from that scene. There he heard a voice that was all too familiar.

"Hey over here, help me," it cries out.

" We got you buddy, hang in there," and once again like so many times before, he heard the deafening explosion.

Pete gasped for breath, as he quickly sat up in his bed with sweat rolling down his face. He then realize what has just taken place. The nightmare has recorded this horrible event, and repeats its nightly performances over and over for years.

" I don't think I can stand one more night in that damn cornfield," he says to himself. When will this ever end? He has spoken to doctors, preachers, even other soldiers, and still this nightmare continues. And so does the drinking. The one thing that has always been there for Pete was the liquor and pain pills. Self-medicating himself to recovery was his way out. It might not be the right thing to do, but it had worked all these years he thought. And why stop now he was thinking.

"Because it ain't working dumb ass," he said aloud. The pain of his leg was bad enough but those dreams, night after night, was driving him insane. And that was a short trip at this point. And this time it happened at his mother's house, as Pete and Millie were staying over for a night or two at Knobby's. They would come back home time to time to see Pete's mother after the passing of his dad, Big Jim. But as far as the nightmares, there was no escape and Pete would have to live with it.

Just then the phone started ringing and Pete made no move to answer it as it continued ringing. Ring after ring, Pete finally picked up the phone, keeping it from awaking his mother. The phone he thought, who in the world would be calling this early in the morning? The only person that knew he was in town was Aileen. Aileen, that's who, she is the only person Pete knew that got up that early every day.

"Hello," Pete said as he wiped his eyes of sleep.

"No, honey you do not fold the eggs, you beat them first," said a person on the phone.

"Hello, hello," said Pete. "Ms. Carrie is that you? "

"Hello Pete, can you hear me? It's Aileen. It's important I talk to you Pete."

"Ms. Carrie can we please use the phone? Aileen has something important to tell me. I'm sorry to interrupt you ladies."

"Pete is that you? How's your mother? Is she doing alright? Please tell her we all miss her at church."

"I sure will Ms. Carrie. Now can I speak to Aileen ma'am?"

"Aileen you call me back and I'll give you this recipe as well Sugar".

"Thank you Ms. Carrie. I'll call you back soon," said Aileen and then quickly went back to Pete and their conversation.

"Pete you won't believe what that crazy brother of mine, Lou, has done now! You won't believe it," said Aileen as she seemed fit to be tied. I'm going to kill him!" she shouted.

"Good morning Aileen. Don't you just love party lines?" laughed Pete.

"That crazy Lou! You won't believe what he did this time!"

"Now hold on sugar lump, what is the problem Aileen? Just slow down and tell me," Pete replied as he sat up in the bed.

"That idiot had Billy Keith selling liquor!"

"What the hell are you talking about?" said Pete. "There ain't no way. Lou ain't that crazy."

"The heck you say. He was caught by the police. Dud stopped the whole thing before it got ugly."

"Dud, what's he doing poking around in our business?" Pete was still mad at Dud and had not talked to him in years.

"He's Lou's nephew too Pete and he cares about him, just like you do," said Aileen. "It's silly that you two boys still haven't talked to each other in all these years. Anyway, Lou was caught putting pint size bottles in Billy Keith's new jacket I just bought him last winter. Dud told me that Lou would have Billy going from store to store delivering his goods to the store owners and his other customers," said Aileen, as she started to cry a little more. "He's eight years old Pete."

"Ok, ok sweetie, where's Billy Keith and Lou now?" said Pete, as he was thinking about the whole matter just not making sense.

"Billy is here, with me. The police brought him home.   I guess Lou is still downtown with Dud. Please Pete, please go down there and help Lou. He's the only brother I got left."

"Ok sweetie I'll see what's going on. How's Billy Keith?"

"He seems to be alright I guess. He was crying that he put Lou in jail. I sure hate that I'm going to have to punish that boy."

"Looks like he has been punished enough."

"I just don't understand my brother at all."

"Well, it will be alright, don't you worry. Just give me a couple of hours. I'll get to the bottom of this and I'll call you back later. Don't you worry," said Pete as he hung up the phone, wondering what the hell was going on. Something didn't sound right.

"My, my," said Ms.Carrie, as she too hung up the phone after listening to the whole conversation.

"What was that all about, family again?" asked Millie as she rolled over to look at the time on the alarm clock.

"You guessed it, my family strikes again," said Pete as he started to get out of the bed looking for his pants and his prosthesis.

"What has Lou done this time?" Millie said as she also started to get up and make some coffee.

"O, nothing much... just using an eight year old boy to help sell his liquor door to door in downtown Burlington," he said.

"What, is he crazy?" she shouted. "All I know is the next time, my next husband is going to be a rich orphan! The heck with all this family stuff," she said with a smile.

"Yes, he is crazy, but he's my uncle as well, so don't worry Millie. I'll be back in a few hours or so. I love you," said Pete, as he blew her a kiss good bye and went in the bathroom to get ready.

"Why would Lou do that," said Millie talking through the door to Pete.

"I have no idea what's going on. The whole thing does not make sense, but I'll find out," he said, as he walked out of the bathroom, grabbed his crutches, blew Millie another kiss goodbye, and made his way out the backdoor.

"Well looky here, if it ain't the second broken down old prizefighter we've seen today," said Johnny Law, as Pete entered the jail house entrance. It had been years since the fight at Pete's Pool Hall but the broken nose and scar that Pete left on Johnny's face was still present.

"Where's Lou?" said Pete to Johnny. Johnny stopped smiling. He knew Pete was serious, and pointed with his coffee cup down the corridor.

"He's down the hall in Dud's office." Johnny slowly stepped back away from Pete, not knowing if Pete was mad enough to hit him or not.

"Don't worry Johnny. I'm not mad at you today, thanks," Pete said as he turned and walked down the hall. He walked toward the conversation coming from Dud's office. Pete could hear the two men talking beyond the open door as he walked into Dud's office.

"Well hey there Pete. Look Lou, look what the cat drug in. What's shaking Pete?" said Dud.

"Let's go home Lou. I came down here to get you. Aileen is worried sick," Pete said.

"O' hell Pete, ain't you going to say hello to your cousin Dud?" said Lou. "He sure helped your old Uncle Lou out today."

"What did he do, curse you out after his thugs beat you up and then had you thrown in jail like he did me?"

"Now you hold on here Pete. You know that's not exactly how that happened. Plus that's been about a hundred years ago and you know it!" Dud shouted.

"Now hold on boys," said Lou. "Let's don't go reopening that kettle of fish. That's all behind us now. Besides, you two are here to help Billy Keith."

"Billy Keith? What in the world are you talking about Lou? Heck, I'm here to get you out of jail."

Dud laughed. "Hell, he ain't in jail Pete," said Dud.

"Well Aileen thinks he is, and so does Billy. So what the heck is really going on here? You two must be up to something."

"Well now look here Pete," said Dud. "Here's the deal. Billy Keith saw dumb ass Lou here selling some spring water to old man Staunton."

"Just like I have done for years. I didn't know the little boy saw me."

"Well anyway," said Dud, "eight year old little Billy Keith thought that was neat. So he started to ask Lou about it and saying things like that's really neat and I wish someday I could do that. So old Lou here called me with this plan of his."

"Yea, I sure did," said Lou. "I thought if Billy was to see me get arrested then that would scare him enough to where we won't have to worry if that boy goes down the straight and narrow path or not. And hell, I think it worked."

"I think so too," said Pete, "but you two are forgetting one very important thing."

"What's that?" the two men said.

"You scared the hell out of everybody else!" shouted Pete.

"I guess you're right, but sometimes you got to shake up things to get them right," said Lou.

"Well you two damn sure did that," as all three men started laughing. "Well let's don't start kissing each other on the lips just yet. I'm still pissed at Dud," said Pete.

"Come on Pete. That's been years ago. Hell I'm the one that lost his job over it, not you. Besides, you did get to beat the shit out of all my men, and as for Johnny Law, well, he's never forgotten that night."

Pete shrugged his shoulders and stared at the floor. "I guess you're right Dud. Hell we're too old to keep this up anyway." The three shook hands and laughter broke out in the jail house once again. And by the way, the plan must have worked. Billy Keith never sold liquor again and Dud and Pete were back on speaking terms, after roughly 22 years.

Chapter 38

Blinky's Boy

TOM O'LEARY, THE FIGHT PROMOTER, and Lou were sitting in the dark gym beside the ring taking a drink out of Tom's flask after everyone had left. The two were discussing the future of Tom's nephews, Nelson and Albert, and their next fights.

"Now look here Lou. I don't care what Pete thinks. All I know is you need to get my boy Nelson in that fight. I don't care if these guys are in with Blinky Palermo or not. Heck I'm in the Irish mob my damn self," said Tom as he paced the floor in front of Lou. "Frankie Ryff or Johnny Saxton... they're both real good fighters and I think my nephew can take either one of them," said Tom.

"Yea they are good fighters alright. Frankie Ryff is the crowd favorite in New York because he wins all the time. And Johnny Saxton was the champion of the world at one time not too long ago. I'd say they are pretty good," said Lou.

"I'm just saying they would help start a good boxing career for both boys, plus my family would be very pleased as well," said Tom.

"Well, the question is, do you really want to deal with Blinky's boys? Do you really want to get involved with all of that?" asked Lou.

Tom looked at him dumbfounded.

"You've got to be kidding me," said Lou. "Don't you understand Tom? They are Palermo's boys. Pete and I don't want to have anything to do with that bunch of thugs."

All of a sudden the lights came on in the gym and there was Pete standing in the corner. He had heard every word and from the look on his face he was not happy. "I told you Lou. I never wanted to see that SOB Tom in here again," said Pete as he was walking toward Lou.

"Now hold on hot head," said Tom. "There's no reason for you to be pissed at me Pete. Lou and I were just talking business, that's all."

"The hell you say," said Pete. "You're a mobster Tom. I don't want you or anyone like you in my gym. And I sure as hell don't want to deal with Blinky Palermo." Pete kept walking closer to the ring side where Tom was standing as he kept talking. "Tom you're bad news and you always have been. I've had it, so you need to get the hell out of here. I mean it."

"Now look here Pete, there's no reason for you to be this mad. Business is business. There's nothing personal here," said Tom.

Pete turned and placed his crutches over in the corner as he walked right up to Tom. "You're going to get your ass whipped Tom if you don't leave," said Pete.

"That's it then," said Tom, as they both put their hands up ready to fight. They started to study one another, sizing up the situation. Pete stood there on one leg while Tom started to circle him.

"Now wait a damn minute!" said Lou. "You two old son of bitches are going to kill each other with a heart attack, not a fistfight. I can't believe you two!"

"Ok, if that's what you want, you old crippled son of a bitch," said Tom as he pushed back the folding chairs to make room for the brawl.

Pete took no time getting over to Tom, and with one powerful left hook Tom was down on the ground, but with the swing of the punch Pete lost his balance and he too went down. They both struggled to get up on their feet. And once again Pete found his target and Tom hit the floor for the second time. But he was a tough old bird himself, and with a little help from the ropes on the ring he pulled himself right back up. This time Tom just kicked Pete in his good leg and down Pete went.

Lou stood there with his mouth open. He could not believe what he was watching. It was like the Friday night fights at the old folk's home. Swinging with all they had as they worked their way back to their feet, they started throwing more air punches, both missing more than hitting. They soon started to get tired, with both of them bent over and trying to catch their breath. Tom turned and picked up one of the folding chairs to hit Pete over the head with it, but he fell down trying to do that. It was a comedy, like watching a saloon fight on the Jackie Gleason show.

"Hold it you two," said Lou, as he grabbed the two of them at the same time. "That's enough of that shit! You two are embarrassing as hell. You look like a couple of wash women beating your laundry. Hell, just pull out a gun and shoot each other or something," said Lou as he tried to move a few chairs back in place.

Both fighters were sitting on the floor, breathing like they both had been in a marathon.

"We're too old to beat each other up," said Pete in between breaths.

"I think we did a pretty good job in a short period of time," said Tom, still trying to breathe. "But if I knew you would grow up to be such a mean old son of a bitch like you are, I would not have saved your ass in that damn minefield," said Tom.

"What did you say?" said Pete.   He was still bent over double. "What the hell are you talking about Tom?"

"You know what I'm talking about Pete, back in Italy in that damn minefield outside Palermo.   That's right, soldier."

"What about Palermo?" said Pete, acting like he didn't know anything.

"That was me. I was the first one of the medics that got to you," said Tom as he started to get off the floor. "And of course we lost three good men trying to save you. Their names were, Thomas Payne, William Benson and James Davis. I bet you didn't know that did you?"

"I cannot believe it was you," Pete said as he started to sit up to see Tom's face.

Tom looked Pete dead in the eyes and said, "We got you buddy, hang in there.   I think I said something like that."

Pete was shocked; he could not believe what he was hearing. After all these years, those were words that had haunted him. He stood on one leg looking for his crutches while his mind was racing. "I just tried to beat up the one man who saved my life all those years ago," Pete was thinking.

"Why didn't you tell me before now?" Pete said, as he looked over at Tom.

"Why, so you would be nice to me?" said Tom. "Hell that was my job then Pete, just like now I'm trying to take care of my family. A man has got to do whatever it takes. That's all it is Pete. Sure I would like for you to like me but that is not going to happen, now is it?"

"No, I guess you're right, but damn Tom, I had no idea it was you," said Pete as the two helped each other to stand upright.

"Well let's don't go kissing each other on the mouth just yet," said Lou. "Tom still wants you to let Nelson fight either Frankie Ryff or Johnny Saxton."

"Ryff, he's a good kid," said Pete. "I don't have a problem with him, but no way on Saxton. He's too close to Blinky. Besides, Nelson is not going to fight either one. I'll need him to help me get Al ready."

"Ready for what?"

"We're going to fight in California."

"California, to fight who?" both Lou and Tom spoke at the sometime.

"Boys, we are going to the Cow Palace to fight Eddie Machen, that's who. That's what I came down here to tell Lou."

"Eddie Machen, not bad, not bad at all," said Lou. "He fits our style and he is a sucker for lefties," Lou said with a little smile.

"You got a problem with him Tom? Sure is a higher rung on the old boxing ladder ain't he?"

"No problem here," said Tom. "That's great. I must say Pete, you really have been looking out for my boys, and I and my whole family appreciates it too. You know Pete, not just anybody could have made it through that minefield like you did. You are one tough son of a bitch. You can't fight worth a shit anymore," he said with a smile, "but you are a tough guy, and you better believe I appreciate everything you have done for those two boys. If there's anything you need you call, ok?" And with that Tom O'Leary got his coat and hat and slowly walked his way out of the gym.

"Ain't that some shit! All this time and it turns out that a mobster kept you from dying in the war," Lou chuckled. "I'll be, ain't life funny."

Pete sat there with a blank look on his face, thinking once again of the men who died trying to save him. And yes, he thought, he did remember their names all these years. Remember, hell he heard their voices almost every night. How could he ever forget them he thought, and he never would.

Chapter 39

Gone, The Legend

MILLIE WAS IN THE KITCHEN hard at cleaning the sink with Borax and dreaming of a dishwasher when Pete entered the front door. He slowly placed his old crutches against the wall and hung his wet overcoat and hat on the hall tree. Millie called from the other room.

"Pete is that you? I'm in here," she said.

"Hey baby it's me," and that's all he said. His silence was always deafening. Sensing something was wrong, Millie came out of the kitchen wiping her hands off on a small towel.

"Pete what is it, where's Lou? You boys are going to miss the plane." He did not say a word. "What's with the long face Pete?"

Pete handed her the afternoon newspaper as he took a seat on the couch, seeming withdrawn from the world. Millie placed her hand over her mouth as she read the headlines: FORMER BOXING LEGEND DIES IN FLORIDA. "O my goodness!" she said as she dropped the paper and looked at Pete.

"It's Lou," Pete said, as the tears welled up in his blood shot eyes. Kicking at the coffee table Pete shouted, "Damn him. I tried to get him to see a doctor. That wonderful old hardheaded S.O.B., I'm going to miss the shit out of him."

Millie bent down and tried to love on her man that was hurting and kissed him on the forehead. The two held hands, and finally Pete looked up and kissed her back. "When did he go to Florida? I thought the two of you were going to San Francisco in a few weeks," she said, as she sat down beside Pete to comfort him.

"No, he told me he had a wife in Ocala and he wanted to patch things up with her. He has been gone for about a month," Pete said. "Nelson and Albert were going with me to San Francisco, but I called it off."

"You can't do that. This fight means the world to both those boys and you too." Millie stood up, placing both hands on her hips, trying to show a sign of strength.

"I'll see about rescheduling that match, but for right now all I can think about is Lou." Pete slowly lowered himself into his favorite chair with a long, sad look on his face. Pete sat thinking of Lou and the days when he was between his boxing career and wrestling promoting and the time he spent with Pete working in the gym together. He remembered the great stories Lou would tell, such as how he would travel the country promoting boxing and wrestling events, to doing odd jobs to panhandling on the city street corners. For years he traveled on the road and worked the streets like a gypsy. He and his faithful dog Buster, all those years on the road and all those little brown and white dogs, and every one of those terriers was named Buster.

"Ok folks gather around and pay attention. Follow the ball as I place it under the cups," Lou would say as the crowd of bystanders grew to see what the commotion was all about. Lou would place the little red ball under the center cup of three and start moving each upside down cup in a circular motion for about twenty seconds or so, stopping just long enough to show the crowd that the ball was still there under the same cup and repeating this several times till he finally stopped. "Ok, where's the ball?" asked Lou to the curious onlookers.

"It's under that one," said the little freckly faced, red headed boy.

"Then place your quarter on the table," said Lou.

The little boy did so, as he kept pointing to the cup in the middle with his other hand. Lou then slowly turned over the cup to show that it was empty.

"O' shoot," said the little boy. "How could I be wrong?"

The crowd that had gathered thought the same. Lou then turned over the other two cups as well and again there was no ball. Throughout the crowd most of the spectators were now wondering where in the world it could be. On cue, little Buster jumped up on top of the little folding table, as order by Lou. He then bent his head down, opened his mouth, and out popped the small red ball. Lou then picked up the ball and showed it to the disbelieving crowd. The crowd started to cheer and the money flowed out of their pockets like rain. Then for an encore, Buster danced for money. Lou placed the customer's dollar in Buster's mouth and for that amount the little terrier, wearing his sunglasses and hat, started spinning and jumping in circles on his hind legs. This would go on until the cops came to break up the crowd that by this time was spilling into the street traffic. Lou and Buster packed up and it was off to another circus tent or street corner, doing whatever it took to make a buck. He loved every minute of it, Pete thought, as he came back to realization of Lou's passing. "P.T. Barnum didn't have anything on old Lou Carpenter, and this world will never see another just like him either," Pete whispered, as the tears of love flowed once again.

Chapter 40

The Left Coast

THE PLANE RIDE TO CALIFORNIA WAS tough on old Pete, hours stuck in the small space, his leg had been bothering him for weeks, plus the passing of Lou was still fresh on his mind. Pete didn't seem to be himself thought Al.

"Come on Pete. Nelson called from the hotel and said the press conference is in a couple of hours. We need to hurry up," said Al.

"I'm coming, I'm coming," Pete said, as he rubbed his leg up and down trying to get the blood to flow better. "What's the hurry? They can't start the fight without you." Pete laughed. "Besides, the fight ain't till Friday night. We got plenty of time, don't worry kid."

After saying all that Pete was worried for the first time in years. He would be ring side without Lou, and this was the fight he had been waiting for his whole life. He finally got one of his boys fighting a big time heavyweight contender in Eddie Machen. The fight between Al and Amos "Big Train" Lincoln never materialized due to dates and bad timing, but this fight was the one Lou always thought would suit Al better. Machen was a cagey fighter, a convict turned boxer from Redding, California, with a lot of time in the ring with the who's who of big time heavyweight champions like Ernie Terrell, "Big Cat" Williams, Sonny Liston, George Huvalo and Zora Folly, just to name a few. He might be a little past his prime but he was still a dangerous fighter.

Pete thought if Al Flynn could only beat Machen this would write his and Pete's ticket to the big leagues. But enough of that kind of thinking. First they would have to beat one of the fourth or fifth heavyweight contenders in the world. Plus it was to be held in his house, the Cow Palace, in Daly City, California, just outside of San Francisco. It was the California State Livestock Pavilion but was known worldwide as the Cow Palace and a great sports arena.

"And that's a long way from Hopedale," Sleepy would say, Pete thought. He was going to miss him on this trip as well. Sleepy had opened a little café, more like a bar, back home when he and his wife got back together. So now he was where she could keep an eye on him, and he could hang out with his buddies at the new bar, telling lies and old war stories.

Pete was standing in the middle of the airport day dreaming when Al came running back to get him. He had hailed a cab for the ride from the airport to the hotel downtown and went back inside to get Pete. "Hey did you bring your coat?" Al asked.

"No, I got my sweater though. Mark Twain always said that the coldest winter he ever endured was a summer in San Francisco, and he's right. It's cold as hell out here!" and they both laughed. Pete suddenly stopped in front of a sign in the airport terminal that read 'Machen vs. Flynn, at the Cow Palace and Sports Arena. Don't miss it.' "Look son there's your name. Now all we got to do is make people remember it," Pete said as he put his arm around Al's shoulders.

"Yes sir, I understand," said Al, as they walked to the waiting cab with the engine running.

"Hey fellows, let me get those bags sir," said the cabbie, as he grabbed the bundles away from Pete and Al and helped Pete into the car. "Awful nice to meet you Mr. Flynn. I've seen your picture all around town. Looking forward to the fight Friday night myself."

"Thanks," said Al, who was a little embarrassed over his new found fame.

The cabbie turned the car out of the parking area, turned on the radio and headed toward downtown. "How about some music," he said, as he turned up the volume on the radio.

"Now Al once we get to the hotel and we get that press conference over we need to head straight to the gym. I've got it all lined up," said Pete.

"I know," said Al, "with one of your old war buddies."

"How did you guess?" said Pete.

"There's always one around," he laughed.

The music on the radio stopped playing. The cabbie looked at the radio like there was something wrong with it, but then the announcer came on the air.

"We interrupt this broadcast for a K.S.F.O. news bulletin. As of 2pm

Pacific time, a spokesperson who handles the Eddie Machen fight team, announced that the fight this Friday night has been cancelled due to a medical issue. Again, I repeat, the fight between Eddie Machen and Albert Flynn that was to be broadcast live on these airwaves this Friday night from the Cow Palace has been cancelled due to medical issues announced from the camp of boxer Eddie Machen. We now return to our regular scheduled programming and back to the music you love here on K. S. F. O.," said the announcer and the music started back where it had left off.

Al and Pete looked at each other, shock registering on their faces. Did they really hear that the fight was cancelled? What kind of medical issues were they talking about? This couldn't be right.

"That's some stuff," said the cabbie, as he slowed down and acted as if he didn't know where to go or what to do.

"Just keep going. Take us to the hotel," said Pete. "We still need to go there."

"Yea, ok, sure thing," said the cabbie, as he picked up his speed once again and headed over the Golden Gate Bridge with both Pete and Al looking at the Pacific coast for the first time, with the city by the bay in the distance.

"You think we can still see the Cow Palace before we head back home Pete?" asked Al.

"See it, hell you're going to fight in it!"

"But Pete, did you not hear the man on the radio," Al said, with a question mark in his voice.

"Yea, I heard him, but that don't mean nothing. You just leave it to me," as he patted Al on the leg. "This might work out better than I thought."

Al smiled back at Pete. "I know. You got an old war buddy," Al chuckled.

"That's right son I do, I do indeed," said Pete with a smile on his face as the cab pulled up the curb in front of the hotel.

Chapter 41

Slowing down Speedy

"I DON'T GIVE A DAMN," said one of the two big men in the dark suits with his hands around Speedy's throat. "You better have our money by next week or your ass is mine. You understand me boy?" the man said, as he pushed Speedy to the floor of the little café diner.

Speedy shook his head in agreement. "Yea I understand alright," he said under his breath as he started to get up. The second man put his foot on Speedy's back and pushed him back to the floor.

"You better look at me boy," he said.   Speedy then rolled over on his back as the large man bent down and looked right in Speedy's eyes. "Don't you make this unpleasant. We don't want to hurt you boy but the man wants what is his," the second man said as he put his foot on Speedy's chest this time. "Do you understand?" he asked again for the second time.

"Yes," said Speedy. "I get it fellows. I understand." That seemed to do the trick and with that the two thugs turned and walked away, leaving Speedy lying on the floor of the diner as they walked away.

"Speedy you want your eggs on the floor or you want me to put them at your booth?" said Nancy, Sam's daughter and waitress, with a laugh in her voice.   She had seen this kind of thing too many times to really worry about it.

Speedy made his way to his feet and dusted himself off as if nothing had happened. "Sure thing doll. Just put the entrée at my favorite table please," he said as he patted her on the bottom and made his way to sit down. Sam's Diner is where Speedy held his place of business for years, ever since he came home from the war and Sam, being a bookie, took him in like his own. And now Speedy was following in Sam's footprints as a two cents bookie himself.

"Great morning ain't it," he said.

"Just lovely.   The birds are chirping, street washers are sweeping and the gangsters are whipping your ass again. All is perfect in the world," she said as she placed the breakfast on the table.

"Well, I can't help that Machen is not going to fight. How can they make me pay for that? They haven't lost any money.   Hell the fight is still three weeks away from this Friday anyway," Speedy said to Nancy as she looked at him like she could care less, chewing her last piece of bubble gum.

"That ain't the problem Einstein," said Nancy. "The problem is you haven't paid them back from the last two fights and last week's horse race and they know you have already spent the money. They just want it back."

"Oh that's how it works. Well ain't you the smartest waitress in all of San Francisco," said Speedy as he started working on his breakfast.

"No, but I am one of the better looking ones I must say," as she walked off.

Speedy looked at her as she walked off. "You got that right," he said, as he eyed her backside sashaying away from him. "Now that's a set of biscuits!"

As Nancy rounded the corner she stuck her head through the opening of the kitchen window. "Hey Speedy, by the way, you got a message from some guy named Pete."

"What?" said Speedy, as he was going to town on the first hot meal he had had in days.

One of the other customers, hearing their conversation turned his stool and repeated, "She said some fellow named Pete called and left a message." The customer then turned his stool back around to face his food.

"Here it is," said Nancy, as she brought out the note, plus more biscuits and gravy for Speedy to attack.

Speedy took the note and stopped eating long enough to read the message: *'Will be in town for a few days for the fights and would love to get together and talk old times. Call me at the Drake downtown, your Buddy Pete Smith.'*

"Well ain't that something," said Speedy aloud, "and I was just wondering if he is still in the fight game," he said as he finished off another biscuit. "That interesting ."

"Speedy who's that?" said Nancy, as she turned from taking an order from a couple of regulars at the bar.

"Just a friend, that's all doll," he said back to Nancy, but to himself he thought, "just a friend that might have just saved my neck. Old Pete just might be a real life saver." Speedy sat back in the booth, feeling more self-confident and feeling a lot better than he did ten minutes ago.

"My boy Pete comes to the rescue once again," he thought as he started to read the morning paper again, after being so rudely interrupted earlier.

Chapter 42

Room of Doom

"SO LET ME GET THIS STRAIGHT, we either fight Doug Jones, the number two heavyweight contender in the world, or your fighter, Thad Spencer, the number one contender on short notice, because Eddie Machen is in the hospital with suicidal thoughts," said Pete standing in his hotel room talking to another person on the phone.

"No you don't have to fight either one Pete," said Willie Ketchum, the promoter and Thad Spencer's manager and trainer, "but the folks at the Cow Palace would appreciate it. They have already lost their shirt on this thing with Machen backing out and were hoping to salvage something by using a draw like Jones or Spencer. Plus the word on the street is that Cassius Clay's WBA belt, I mean Ali, will be given to the winner of an up and coming eight man elimination tournament. And as of right now my boy is in with a win over Jones or any other big contender, but I need to keep him sharp. There's where you and your boy come in."

Pete kept pacing the floor of his hotel with his crutch in one hand and the telephone in the other. "Machen has suicidal thoughts? Hell he doesn't have to fight those two, and for all I know my boy might be in the same hospital ward with Machen after he finds out about this lineup."

"Calm down Pete. First of all we will reschedule the fight so you and your boy will have two more weeks to train, plus the Cow Palace will pick up your tab for the hotel and all accommodations," said Ketchum. "It's going to be fine."

"When will we know who and how much time we got to respond?"

"I'll call you back in a couple of days. That should give you enough time to think about it and talk it over with your people," and with that Ketchum hung up the phone.

"Well that's some kind of deal," Pete thought. "My boy ain't got a snowball's chance in hell with those two bombers, Jones or Spencer. That's not exactly who you want to cut your teeth on," Pete said aloud.

The door of Pete's hotel room opened and in walked Al and Nelson, both looking like something was terribly wrong. The brothers kept looking down at the floor as they walked in the room, neither one saying a word.

"Damn boys, you look like you two have lost your best friend. What's wrong?" asked Pete.

No one said a word for the longest time; the room was full of silence. Then Nelson spoke. "OK, It's the war," Nelson said.

"The war? Ok the war of what?" said Pete.

"You know, the war, Pete, the Vietnam War, the damn war that's going on in South East Asia, the one that's on the TV news every night," Nelson shouted.

"OK, what about it? Is it over? What about it?" Pete said with a questionable look on his face.

"No Pete, Al has been drafted to go to war," said Nelson, as he turned to show Pete a piece of paper. "He just got his draft notice."

Al stood there without saying a word as Pete looked at him and the paper Nelson just handed him. "You have got to be shitting me! Drafted? How the hell did you get drafted?" Pete looked at the paper again. "Drafted," he repeated. "Are you sure this is real? Come on boys you're pulling my only good leg, right? I'm too old for this shit and you two know better than to do this to me." Pete looked at both boys for an answer, but the two said nothing.

Pete started pacing the floor and talking to himself. "You've got to be kidding," said Pete walking back and forth. "This is the most screwed up trip I have ever been on in my life! What the hell is going to happen next?" And as if on cue the telephone rang. Pete quickly turned toward the ringing phone. "Whoever that is can't be good," thought Pete as he slowly walked over and grabbed the ringing phone.

"Hey Pete, it's Speedy. What's shaking old buddy?"

"Speedy, I can't talk to you right now. Let me call you back. I'm in the middle of something. I'll call you right back." Pete hung up the phone.

"Look Pete I'll fight," said Al.

"Fight!" shouted Pete. " Did you see the date on this notice? Hell you have to report to the Army in two days son, two days," said Pete as he sat down on the couch with his face in his hands. He then looked over at Al who was sitting over at the table with his face in his hands as well. "Hey Al," said Pete as he got up and walked over to his fighter and put his hand on his shoulder. "Don't you worry about some dumb fight son. You have a real fight coming in a couple of days. You need not to worry about old Pete. You need to get ready to serve your country."

Al looked back at Pete. "I don't know about all that Pete. I've been thinking about Canada."

"Canada? I did not hear that, no sir. If Uncle Sam wants you Al, you best be going to see Uncle Sam. That's all I'm saying."

"But Pete," said Nelson.

"Don't you get involved too Nelson. This is Al's deal and Al only. Uncle Sam doesn't play boys. That's all I have to say about it. I mean it Al; it's your ass and no one else's. You two understand?"

"Yes sir," the two said together. "We understand Pete."

"I've got to get out of here. This room is bad luck," and Pete turned, grabbing his crutches and shaking his head in disbelief as he left the hotel room headed for the elevator.

"Thanks Pete, thanks for everything," said Al, standing in the doorway of his hotel room. The elevator door opened and Pete stepped in and turned and saw Al as the doors were about to close.

"You are welcome son. It's been my pleasure," said Pete as the doors of the elevator closed.

Chapter 43

Nancy's Plan of Attack

SPEEDY SAT STARING AT THE PHONE on the wall of the café, wondering if and when Pete would call back. The regular crowd was finishing their lunch as a few tourists were still standing at the counter reading the big overhead menu. Speedy was in deep thought, thinking how he could get Pete to help with his gambling debt situation. There has to be a better way than asking Pete's boy to take a dive. But how else could Pete help? I'll just have to come up with something better than that, he thought.

About that same time he heard the bell over the door ring as a new customer entered the diner. "Can't a fella get any service around here?"

"Yes sir, I'll be right with you," said Nancy as she quickly came out from the kitchen.

Speedy quickly turned, and there he saw his old war buddy standing in the door way. "Pete you old son of a gun," said Speedy, as he got up from his office booth to give his friend a warm greeting and hug. "Damn Pete, you ain't changed a bit. You look great buddy. How's everything?

Here have a seat," as he pointed to his booth.

"Hey Nancy, this is my old Army buddy Pete Smith. He's the one I was telling you about. Be sure you get this man anything he wants. He's buying," laughed Speedy.

"Nice to meet you young lady," said Pete as he and Speedy took a seat in Speedy's office. Pete placed his crutches beside the booth.

"I still can't believe that happened to you. I have felt like the biggest asshole about that every day for all these years since it happened," said Speedy. "It should have been me on that patrol that night, not you. If you had not been covering for me, mainly because I had been out drinking, you would have never been hurt and I am so sorry Pete," said Speedy as he reached out and grabbed Pete's hand.

"Ok, it's ok Speedy. I'm good and yes it's good to see you too asshole. Now what's with the shake down Speedy? I know you and you've never felt bad about that night. Hell you're the one that told me I was a fool to go out that night anyway, so what's up with you? What's this all about? How much shit are you into?"

"Well I guess I couldn't shake you old friend. You see its Nancy. She's sick and needs an operation."

Pete looked at his old buddy and started to get up from his seat. "Wait, Pete. Where are you going? You just got here." Speedy reached out with his hand to stop him.

"Look here old friend, we have been through too much shit together for you to start lying to me now. So you either tell me how much money you owe some flat nose thug or I'm out of here and this time for good. Do you understand me?"

Speedy looked down at the floor, not knowing what to say. Pete was right as rain on all accounts. Speedy was too embarrassed to argue; Pete was right and he knew it.

"It's Blinky," said Speedy as he lifted his head up and looked Pete square in the eyes. "Blinky Palermo, he's the one. I owe the money to Blinky Palermo the gangster. Do you know him Pete? He's a bad man and he is going to hurt or kill me if I can't come up with something and something quick," said a meek and mild Speedy Kramer.

"Yea, I know that S.O.B.. Are you kidding, everyone in boxing knows Blinky and you're right. He is a bad man. Speedy you do not want to mess around with a cat like Palermo. He doesn't play. If you owe him money you need to pay up. Don't try to mess around. He ain't the kind to mess with Speedy, understand me?"

"I understand Pete, but it's a lot of money, money I don't have and will never have. It's a lot."

The two men sat back in their seats without saying a word. Customers came and went and the two of them sat there thinking on a plan of attack for the situation.

"Hey you two motor mouths want some coffee?" said Nancy as she stood there with a pot of coffee and couple of cups in her hands.

"Oh yea sweetheart, that would be great, thanks," said Speedy as he seemed to awake from a year long coma.

"You know Speedy, I've been thinking," said Nancy. "You can't pull the wool over the eyes of those gangsters. Why don't you join with them, or make them think you are working for them. You'll get killed if you back stab those kinds of folks. If I were you I would be straight up with them. Heck your friend Pete is a trainer, so well, go train. Being smarter ain't hard to do. They aren't too brainy, if you know what I mean," she said pointing at her head with her pencil.

"That's a great idea. Speedy do you know anyone in the Thad Spencer camp? You know the boxer?" said Pete.

"Yea I know a couple of folks over there Pete. Why?"

"Don't know just yet, but I'm thinking on something," said Pete as he grabbed up his hat and crutches and quickly leaned over and kissed Nancy on the lips. "Speedy you need to marry this girl. She's great."

"But Pete, where are you going? We haven't talked for years."

"Yea sorry about that, but if Nancy is right, I need to work fast. We don't have much time before that fight and if all goes well I just might be able to get you out of this mess."

"But Pete," said Speedy.

"You just sit tight Speedy and kept your fingers crossed.   I'll give you a call soon". And with that Pete was gone with the wind.

"For someone on crutches, he sure gets around pretty good, and they call you Speedy," Nancy said with a laugh as they both sat there in the cafe watching Pete as he drove off in a cab.

Chapter 44

Welcome Aboard

PETE STOOD IN THE CORNER OF THE GYM, watching the two boxers in the ring going at each other. No one seemed to notice or care as Pete watched every move of the more powerful and skillful boxer as he worked over his opponent.

So that's Thad Spencer, he thought to himself as the match went on. He also noticed his breathing was shallow and his hands were hanging low. This man is out of shape Pete realized and he had no doubt his boy Al would eat this guy up. It was a shame he would not get that chance Pete thought, as the sparing of the men played out in the ring.

"Hey you, this is a closed gym. You are not supposed to be in here mister," said one of the handlers from ringside.

"You need to leave. You can't stay in here," said another.

Pete stepped out of the shadows from the back of the gym. "Hey Willie, looks like your boy is a little out of shape, but not too bad. He's still got good control with his jab and his foot work looks good as well," said Pete. He now seemed to have gotten everyone's attention. Even the boxers stopped their workout and all eyes were on Pete.

"Pete Smith is that you?" said Willie Ketchum, Thad Spencer's manger, as he worked his way down from the ring to get closer to Pete. The two men shook hands as they met together at the foot of the steps along ring side. Pete and Willie were friends for years. They went way back to the time Willie's fighter, Featherweight Champion of the World, Davey Moore, was killed after suffering from a fatal brain injury. Willie was out of the fight game for a long time, but now with Spencer, Ketchum was back and back to his old winning ways.

"You told me to come by so here I am," said Pete.

"Everybody, I want you the meet one of the best trainers in the business. Thad, this is Pete Smith from North Carolina. Pete, what the heck are you doing here? I figured you boys had picked up and headed back home by now."

"No, everyone else has but to tell you the truth Willie, since I was here in town I thought I would stay and see you guys get that Doug Jones fight. I don't have much to do now that my boy has been drafted. I still can't believe that mess."

"I can't believe that either," said Ketchum . "I'm so sorry for Al, and you guys. Damn that's something else. Is there anything I can do to help you? Just ask."

"Well, believe it or not, that's why I'm here. You see Willie, I got an old war buddy that needs some help. And well, anyway I want to offer you my services if and only if you think I could help. Not taking anything from you Willie, but I think I really could teach Thad here a couple of things that might help you guys beat Doug Jones. What do you say?"

"Wow that was out of the blue," said Willie. "Doug Jones and Thad Spencer... that would be a good one, no doubt about it. What do you say Babe?" Willie turned to Thad. "You think you need some help? You think Pete here can help us out a little bit?"

"More the merrier," said Thad. "Sure thing, I could always use more help Mr. Ketchum," as he reached down from the ring and shook Pete's hand. "Welcome aboard Mister Smith," he said in a deep voice. "Welcome aboard."

"All righty then, I'll just go check out of the hotel and get my things. You don't mind if I stay here at the gym? It reminds me of back home."

"I think that will be just fine," said Willie as he patted Pete on the back. "We're still hoping for that fight for the WBA title. As of right now it looks like its Floyd Patterson, Ernie Terrell, Oscar Bonevena, Jimmy Ellis, Jerry Quarry, Joe Frazier, and Karl Mildenberger from Germany. So a lot is on the line with this fight Pete. This kid is a diamond in the rough, but he's got issues," said Willie as he and Pete walked away so Thad could not hear them.

"Hell Willie, all fighters have an issue. That's why they need us," and the two men laughed. "Plus we need to focus on this fight first with Jones. Let's get through this one, ok?"

"Sure thing Pete. Again, I'm glad you are here. Welcome aboard. I'll see you first thing in the morning."

Chapter 45

Room Guest

AS PETE ARRIVIED AT HIS HOTEL ROOM he saw he was not alone. He noticed the door was ajar and he heard voices inside the room. He quickly turned and started to head back to the elevator but stopped when he heard another voice right behind him.

  "Hey Mister Smith, would you like to come inside? After all it is your room," said the big man with a raincoat on and his right hand inside the coat pocket pointing at him.

  "Sure thing buddy, whatever you say," said Pete as he decided to go back to his room on second thought.

  "Well if it ain't Mr. Pete Smith, the fantastic one-legged boxing trainer," said the man with a thick European accent. He was an older, very thin man sitting in a chair in front of the window. All you could see of him was his silhouette as the sun's light came in through the room's window. "Nice view you got here Mr. Smith," as he turned and looked out the sliding door to the balcony. He took a cigarette out of his pocket and quickly one of his henchmen was fast on the draw to light it for him. "Care for a smoke Pete? I can call you Pete, can't I?" he asked.

  "Sure you can call me Pete, but no I don't care for a smoke, and yes it is a nice view, Mr. …?"

"Let's just say I'm a friend of a friend and let's just leave it at that ok?" said the thin man. "But what is more important is why I'm here and for you to realize your friend, Mr. Kramer, is in a deep, deep situation, if you understand my meaning."

"I do understand his problem. I just don't understand why you are making it my problem," said Pete as he tried to walk over closer to get a better view of Mr. Thin who was sitting straight across from Pete on the other side of the room. One ganger walked over and stopped Pete from getting any closer to his boss.

"Now Pete, don't get upset. We have no intention of hurting you. Please don't feel threatened. I assure you of that. We just want to know, in your opinion, who you think is the better fighter, Thad Spencer or Doug Jones?"

"What, why would you ask me? Don't you subscribe to Ring magazine," he said with a laugh and there was no laughter in return. "Ok that's easy, it's Doug Jones, by far," said Pete as he looked around the room to make sure he kept everyone where he could see them.

"Are you sure of that?"

"Yes I'm sure. He's more experienced, plus he's got a better punch count, a better trainer and of course a better fight record. So on all accounts, in my opinion; he is the better fighter hands down."

"Yes, but like in life Pete, the better man does not always win, nor does he leave the battlefield in war in one piece, now does he?" said the thin man with a smile on his face. "Look here Pete. Your friend Speedy owes me and my associates a great deal of money. And let's just say if you could work a little magic and make sure the right fellow wins this fight we might see our way of letting him off the proverbial hook. Do you understand me?"

Pete was not sure what to do. He did not want to mess things up by pissing off the mob nor, in turn, did he want to get Speedy or himself hurt in doing something dumb. Plus there were five against one, not bad odds for Pete in his hay day, but this was for more than just Pete's pride on the line and he knew it. Pete walked over and grabbed his bag that was packed and sitting on the floor beside the bed, and turned to the old, thin man sitting in the chair.

"I understand," Pete said, shaking his head. "I also understand you gentlemen are in my room, and in my room uninvited, I might add, but since I was checking out anyway, I guess it's not really my room, not any more, is it? So I guess I'll just leave you gentlemen here in hopes that the room is to your liking. O' and by the way, since I just took a job in Thad Spencer's camp I would tell your associates to bet the farm on him. Because after I get through getting his ass in shape, there ain't no way in hell he'll get beat. And as far as my friend Speedy, I have a few friends in your line of business as well, so I hope in your case nothing bad happens to him. Do you understand me old man? Two can play at this game. And I'm too tired and too old to put up with your gangster shit. I'm sure I'll see you on fight night." Pete was stopped on his way out by one of the thugs before he could leave the room.

"Well Pete, looks like I underestimated you and I appreciate a man with your gumption , but the bottom line is this; if your man does not win that fight your friend Speedy will not be around to see the winner. "

"Fine, I'll see you ring side on fight night," said Pete and he then gave a hard brush off to one of the goons on his way out. The thin man raised his hand to call off his dogs and no one moved.   Pete was out the door.

"Well, was that to your liking?" said the thin man, as the bathroom door opened and out walked Tom O'Leary. He stood there knowing he helped Pete for the last time, and now they were even.

Chapter 46

Bar Rescue

THE CAB PULLED UP IN FRONT OF A REAL ROUGH LOOKING pool hall, in one of the worst areas in Oakland, and slowly Pete and Speedy got out of the cab. The cab idled, without moving.

"Hey buddy you sure you want me to leave?"said the cabbie. "This is a tuff place for your kind, if you know what I mean." Pete pulled a hundred dollar bill out of his pocket, tore it in half and handed one half of it to the waiting driver.

"Good idea. You wait here and we'll be out in twenty minutes and then you'll get the rest," said Pete as he turned to Speedy.

"Hey Pete, when you told me that we're going to be a part of Thad Spencer's team you didn't tell me we would be on booze, drugs, and rescue detail every night. This is about the fifth bar we've been to in about three nights. Man, this kid loves to have fun and in some rough ass parts of town I might add!"

"O stop your bitch'en. We were told to come here and get him, plus if you hadn't gotten in that mess with those mobsters we wouldn't be in this crap in the first place. Now get your ass inside. It's cold as ice cream out here," as he pushed on Speedy to hurry up.

"Yea, yea, I'm going, but say, you never told me the deal you made with Blinky's boys," said Speedy as they walked down a couple of stairs and entered the noisy bar.

"It's all good. Let's get in and get warm. I'll tell you later. Come on."

As they walked in, the place went silent, just like back in the day at old Pete Hall's place, back home on Rawhut Street, and with the same clientele but rougher. The only noise was that of laughter and giggles which seemed to be coming from the back room of the bar. Thinking that must be their boy, Pete and Speedy headed in that direction till someone stuck a leg out to stop them from going any further.

"Hey man, you boys from out of town?" said one of the locals. The rest of the locals started to laugh.

"We're with Thad," said Speedy. "He's got to train tomorrow for the big fight."

"Thad, who the hell is that?" replied the local. "We don't know any Thad."

Pete looked down at the local. "Look sir, we're here to get 'Babe' Thad Spencer, the boxer, and get him in shape for the fight. Now excuse us." Pete used his crutch to push the man's leg out of the way and headed to the back of the bar.

"Well you go right ahead big man, damn," said the local, looking about half pissed. "He's a pretty bad man to be on crutches," the local said under his breath.

Pete and Speedy kept going towards the back hoping the Babe was to be found. All the while, being eyeballed by the local residents, Pete and Speedy made their way through the curious crowd to the back of the bar. As they turned the corner to the sounds of giggles and laughter there was the Babe, entangled with several ladies of the evening. It looked as though they were having their way with young Thad Spencer as they surrounded the heavyweight contender in the back booth of the bar. He was about to go down in more ways than one.

"Hey Babe how's the drinks?" said Pete as he and Speedy walked over and stood between a couple of girls and Thad. Thad looked up from the booth, sandwiched between a couple of ladies.

"Pete, is that you, what the hell, man? Every time I'm having fun you two assholes seem to show up," said Thad as kept kissing on a couple of the ladies and struggling to get his pants back on. He finally stood up on his own power. "Yea man, you need to tell Willie Ketchum to stop checking up on me. Now what are you doing in here Pete," said Thad, holding a girl in one hand and a glass of scotch in the other. "We ain't at no gym, and this right here, this is on my time. Besides they don't like white country folks in here, hillbilly."

Pete stood there taking the abuse, and then he turned towards the women. "Ladies you are going to have to excuse us. Mr. Spencer needs his rest, and this isn't the kind of training he needs with a big fight coming up and all." The girls started to complain, so Pete pulled out his wallet and started handing them some money. "Now, now don't worry. After the big old fight you girls can feel free to have your way with him. Ain't that right Babe?"

"What? Are you crazy old man? I ain't going with you or nobody else. You understand me?" About that time Pete helped the young lady out of the grip of Thad's powerful hands and slowly moved her out of the way. He had earlier handed Speedy his crutch, and like a flash, without warning Pete Smith unlashed of one of his crushing blows that came out of nowhere and caught Thad right on the button with a hard right cross, and down into a drunken heap went the Babe.

The girls started screaming. "Now, now girls, be calm. He's ok," said Pete. As Pete bounded around on one leg trying to balance himself he reached out for his crutch from Speedy.

"Damn Pete, you knocked him out!"

"Shut up Speedy. Don't make too much noise." Pete turned and looked over to see if the other side of the bar had any idea what was going on.

In a whisper Speedy replied, "Yea but he is one of the top heavyweight contenders in the world," as he reached down to catch Thad and help get him up.

"No, right now he's a drugged up drunk, who just got suckered punched. Now come on and help me get this fool out of here. We got some training to do."

"Ok James Braddock, but how the hell do you intend for the two of us, one of which is on crutches, to get this two hundred pounder dead weight of a drunk the hell out of here without being killed by that mob out there?"

Pete quickly pulled out his wallet again. "How would you girls like to make a couple more bucks? Grab a leg and arm."

"Hey where the hell do you think you two are going with the champ," said one of the locals.

Pete looked over at him and a couple of more inquisitive guys standing there with dumb looks and pool sticks. They obviously didn't see Pete hit Thad and definitely would not believe that this old man on crutches could do any damage to a heavyweight prizefighter. "I think he has had a little too much to drink," said Pete. "But you know how he loves the ladies."

"We're going to help him home if that's ok with you gentlemen," said Speedy.

"Sure thing, we don't give a shit," said the local. "Thad drinks up all the cold beer anyway," and they all started laughing.

Pete got Thad's hat and coat, Speedy grabbed his legs and the girls got the rest. Thad was carried to the waiting cab as the whole gang wrestled him in the car and he slept right through it. Off to the gym the three went.

A few hours later Willie Ketchum arrived at the gym. He walked in and as he turned on the lights he saw Pete and Speedy, who had been up all night talking friendship and war stories throughout the evening. "Hey fellows, is everything ok?" asked Ketchum as he saw the two sitting in the dark.

"Everything is fine boss. Your boy is in the back room sleeping it off," said Pete, as he and Speedy slowly got up and walked over to Thad's manager. Pete set his suitcase on the ground beside ringside in the gym. Willie looked down, then back up to Pete, then over to Speedy for an answer.

"What's with this? The fight is not till tomorrow night. Where are you going Pete?"

"My work here is done. That kid is a great boxer Willie. As long as you keep him on track you folks will be fine. Besides you have a great trainer, and Speedy will be here as well."

"Yea, but I need you to keep doing what you do best Pete and that's to keep his mind straight. He loves you guys."

"Hell Willie, I've been nothing but a babysitter. I've been out here in California two months too long. My wife Millie has called me about everyday asking when I was coming home, and I think now's the time. I know you got this fight. He won't have a problem with Jones; your problem will be the fights between you and him trying to keep him straight. I tell you Willie, he is a handful. That boy loves the ladies and likes to party too damn much. I still think he can be a great fighter if you can get his head in the game, and I wish you luck with that."

Willie put his hand on Pete's shoulder. "Thanks for everything Pete. You don't know how much we appreciate it, "said Willie, as he patted Pete on the back and tried to help with his luggage.

"I've got it," said Speedy as he grabbed the bags away from Willie. And together they walked outside to the curb and waited for the cab they had called for earlier.

"You will be fine Speedy. Willie here ain't going to let us down, and our boy is going to win that fight," said Pete as the cab pulled up to the curb.

Speedy put his hand on Pete's shoulder and looked at his friend with appreciation.

"You know Pete, you did it again just like when you saved my life all those years ago in Sicily. If you had not switched duties with me that night, I would not have made it back. I'm not as strong as you and you would still have your boxing career."

"Switch? We had to, you were dead drunk. Someone had to replace your butt! Besides Speedy, you would have done the same thing, if not for me, it would be Bill, Howard, even Sleepy, well maybe not Sleepy," and they both laughed. The boys in Nellie Bell stick together, that's what we do. And that's what I have just done on this trip and would do it again if need be. Hell Speedy I'm still standing. It would take more than that to take me down. Not much more, but more," and the two laughed, helping to hold back the tears.

"I know, that it would Sergeant, that it would." Speedy knew the real reason Pete was leaving before the fight, and that's because he could not stand to see anything happen to his best old war buddy, but it's in God's hands now, not Pete's.

"It was great seeing you again old friend. Now don't you worry about those goons. Hell Pete, I've been dodging those kinds of guys my whole life. But regardless of the circumstances, I'm sure glad we got to be together after all these years Sergeant," said Speedy as he put out his hand to shake Pete's.

"Good times always Speedy," Pete said as the two men hugged and said their goodbyes for the last time.

Chapter 47

Back Home for Good

"AND THAT'S IT SPORTS FANS, Thad Spencer wins over Doug Jones in an exciting ten rounder with a unanimous decision scored by the referee Jack Downie and the two judges in tonight's heavyweight bout here at the Cow Palace in Daly City, California," said the radio announcer, as Pete, sitting in the dim lit room leaned over to put out his cigar and reached up and turned off the radio.

"Well it looks like old Babe Spencer will make the elimination tournament for the WBA belt after all," said Pete as he drank his last drop of Blatz beer.

The eight man elimination tournament did take place and Thad Spencer defeated Ernie Terrell in a nine rounder. In an upset Jimmy Ellis defeated Leotis Martin, who took Joe Frazier's place when Frazier refused to be a part of the tournament. After all, he was the contender and didn't need to fight his way in for the title. Jerry Quarry in a mild upset defeated Floyd Patterson and Oscar Bonevena beat Karl Mildnberger. In the second round of the elimination tournament Ellis once again surprised everyone and beat Bonevena. And that's when Willie Ketchum really needed Pete's help because Thad was beaten badly by Quarry and it

*looked as if the girls and booze won out. Thad "Babe" Spencer was
never the same boxer. His time had come and gone. Ellis, the perpetual
underdog of the tournament, beat Quarry and won the WBA belt. Later
he, too, would be beaten by the number one contender from Beaufort,
South Carolina, "Smokin" Joe Frazier, which would lead up to the much
anticipated fight between Frazier and Mohammed Ali.*

Pete sat back in his chair to reflect on the fight and his trip to the
west coast. It made him tired just thinking about all that had happened.

"I knew that boy would win, and thank God, that means Speedy is
off the hook," he said to himself with a smile on his face. "Now let's see
if old Thad can stay away from the partying long enough," Pete thought,
as he found himself a little melancholy, deep in thought on boxing and
Lou and his life in general. He sat there for what seemed to be hours,
moving and twisting in his chair just enough to settle his stomach with
heartburn from the beers and Reuben sandwich. "I eat too late," he
thought. He then heard the sound of a truck at the front door. "It must
be the milkman," he thought, as he knew it was time to go to bed. He
reached over and grabbed his crutches, looking one more time at the
radio as if he was going to hear more of the fight. But it was over and it
was time to give up the ghost and take it to bed. He moved around
slowly as he passed by the clock in the living room. It was nearly five
o'clock in the morning; the fight was over at two. Pete was still on west
coast time so it was no bother to him. Staying up wasn't the problem
but he was more than ready to go to bed so he could lay next to his
Millie. Pete looked in the bedroom and saw her in a deep, restful sleep,
and looking very content in knowing her man was home. Pete worked
his way around the bedroom placing his crutches in the corner next to
his bed and slowly and carefully he moved under the covers, trying not
to wake her. He patted her on the arm and she made a little smile with
her lips but was still asleep. Pete, too, closed his eyes hoping his
heartburn would calm down as his head lay softly on the pillow, while
his brain was still swirling after the long flight home a couple of days

ago. So much had happened in such a short time he thought... Al going to the Army, working or babysitting Spencer so he would be ready for the fight, and then there's Speedy with his situation.

"What a whirlwind trip. I'm too old for this stuff." He slowly drifted off to a dream state as his mind took him on a journey back to memories of all those friends and family members that had left their indelible mark and impression on Pete, from his parents to his aunts, Aileen and Knobby, to cousins Dud and Lloyd, to his dear friends Sleepy, Speedy and last but not least, Uncle Lou. Lou was the driving force behind Pete's love for boxing and learning to enjoy life in general, and boy did he enjoy it. But it took every one of these wonderful characters of life to do their part in making Pete the man he had become. And of course Millie, the love of his life, Millie was always there by his side helping him cope through all the years of pain, with the loss of his leg and dealing with the horrors of war, through night after night of heart pounding nightmares, to where now those visions comfort him to the point that they are missed if they are not visited soon enough in his nightly dreams. He had adapted, by turning that fear he had when he lost the ability of boxing in the ring, by becoming a prominent part of the sport itself. He did it for years, running a gym, training great amateur Golden Gloves, as well as starting dozens of pro careers, along with inventing several pieces of boxing equipment that they still use today. And it was all out of love; Pete truly loved everything about the sport he was involved in for over forty years. But the one constant throughout his life was his family, the rock that never moved off its foundation. It's that great pillar of love and support one gets through their family's love. Good, bad or indifferent, family and friends have the most input on your life, and truly count the most Pete thought as he then turned over and over in bed trying to get comfortable and thinking, " what a great life I have had!"

That would be his last thought, as the pain quickly swept over his chest, but he went to his rest knowing that Speedy, Sleepy and the rest of his family were going to be ok, now that he is in God's hands.

"Hey Buddy, wake up. It's about time to get a little road work in. You don't want that old Hard Rock Harden to whip your butt again do you?" Pete opened his eyes and there was Uncle Lou, looking to be about thirty five or forty years old again with a towel hanging around his neck, a beer can in one hand and a cigar in the other. And jumping up and down was little Buster, the dog, dancing at his feet.

Pete sits up straight in the bed. "No sir, Uncle Lou, I'm up, I'm up," said Pete as he opened his eyes and arose from the cot in the backroom of the old gym. He turned and put both feet on the cold gym floor and thought to himself, " Old Hard Rock Harden won't know what hit him."

THE END

Acknowledge

I would like to acknowledge some of the men named in the book and others who are listed in the Carolina's Boxing Hall of Fame in Charlotte, North Carolina and on their website, www.carolinasboxinghalloffame.com . The site is full of great stories of men throughout the country that literally fought their way out of hard times. The whole reason for this book was to tell their story and hopefully pay tribute to their hard work and sacrifice. The dedication these men had to the sport of boxing is immeasurable, and their need to be recognized has been long past due. The more you read about these men along with the other nameless boxers; I hope your respect for both them and the sport of boxing will rise.

List below are a few of these men;

LOU KEMP

A Greek immigrant, Lou was the Godfather of amateur boxing on the Charlotte sports scene for nearly 50 years. A former pro bantamweight, Lou made his living working high steel construction but his passion was training young men. He produced many champions including four time world amateur and Olympian Bernard Taylor, heavyweights Neil Wallace, Waban Thomas and Olympian Calvin Brock, future world pro bantamweight champion Kelvin Seabrooks and many more. It is estimated his boxers won over 1,000 amateur matches.

EDWART "HARDROCK" HARDEN

Born April 10, 1910, Graham, N.C. – Boxed 152 amateur and professional – boxed amateur while attending Elon College – Harden had a sensation professional boxing career, was managed by John Loy of Asheville, N.C. – boxed many top heavyweight contenders, Joe Dundee, Al Massey, Red Barry, Mickey O'Brian, Terry Roberts, Joe Lipps, Dewey Kimbrey – At the peak of Harden's career, Jack Dempsey wanted Harden to come to New York and box but Harden declined the offer.

F.W. "GUNNER" OHLANDT JR.

He was an amateur champion having fought 114 bouts and losing only 3. These three losses were later avenged in later bouts. In 1947 he won the Southern Conference Heavyweight Championship. In 1948 he won the same title. In 1950 he was Most Outstanding Boxer at the Southern Intercollegiate Boxing Tournament.

He captained the Citadel Football and Boxing teams and was a member of the Citadel Athletic Hall of Fame. He was Boxing Commissioner in Charleston County for 15 years.

In 1950 he was selected for the "Who's Who" in American Universities and Colleges. Now serving on the Committee for the Hibernian Society in Charleston, S.C., he is also a member of the Board of Directors and has served as President and Vice President of the Executive Association of Greater Charleston.

He has been nominated to the South Carolina Athletic Hall of Fame.

BOB "BOBCAT" MONTGOMERY

Bob "Bobcat" Montgomery, a native of Sumter, South Carolina, had one of the most storied boxing careers in the history of American boxing. In his professional career, Montgomery had a total of 97 fights. Of that, he had 75 wins, which included 37 knockouts, 19 losses and 3 draws. Montgomery began boxing in Battle Royales. Seeing more opportunity up north, the South Carolina native moved to Philadelphia, where he started fighting the likes of Lou Jenkins and Sammy Angott. Montgomery went undefeated in his first 23 fights, going 22-0-1 and winning the Pennsylvania State Lightweight Title.

Three times, Montgomery beat Julie Kogon. Their first fight was at the Broadway Arena in Brooklyn on January 28, 1941, which Montgomery won by decision. They fought again on October 24th that same year, this time at the Chicago Coliseum, a fight Montgomery again took by decision. The two squared off for the last time on June 2, 1947 in Kogon's hometown at the New Haven Arena, but the result was still the same.

At Shibe Park on July 7, 1942, Montgomery lost to former lightweight champ Sammy Angott in a split decision. In 1942, Montgomery had two battles with Maxie Shapiro. In the first fight Montgomery lost by decision in Philadelphia, but he won the rematch two months later by unanimous decision in the same arena.

Montgomery also beat Petey Scalzo by TKO in Philadelphia, but he lost to Al "Bummy" Davis at Madison Square Garden by KO.

On May 21, 1943, Montgomery battled Georgia shoe shiner named "Beau Jack" for the lightweight title. Beau Jack was one of the toughest fighters of the day, but it was Montgomery who won in a 15-round decision. In the rematch, Beau Jack took the title back, but in the rubber match, Montgomery won the title back from Beau Jack. Fights with Ike Williams and Beau Jack set Montgomery apart as one of the all-time greatest fighters in American history.

And the fight Montgomery will always be known for was the WAR BOND FIGHT in 1944 at Madison Square Garden in New York City. Even though Bob lost the fight to Beau Jack, the country was the real winner, as the fight raised $35 million dollars for the U.S. Army.

In 1995, Montgomery was inducted into the International Boxing Hall of Fame.

Montgomery was a promoter at the end of his career.

H.L. "MATTY" MATTHEWS

Were it not for a love of coaching youngsters and WWI, Matty Matthews might have become a major league baseball player. He played in the minor leagues for several years, and some say he was big league material. Matthews was born on Feb. 14, 1889. He began boxing in the Army in 1917. After giving up baseball and his work as a stock broker telegrapher, he became the boxing, baseball and track coach at The Citadel in 1926. He remained on the job for 47 years. As a boxing coach, his team won the Southern Conference title in 1941 and 1948. During his Citadel career, he coached Golden Gloves teams as well. Several of his protégés are members of the Carolinas Boxing Hall of Fame, including Burke Watson, Gunther Ohlandt, Jr., Louis Lempesis, and Harry Hitopoulos. He served as Charleston Boxing Commissioner for a time was known and loved for the advice and guidance he was always willing to share with young athletes. His boxers were known throughout the South as "Mattymen." They knew little of his baseball prowess. They remember him as the best coach who ever showed a kid how to feint with his left.

He and his wife Elsa reared four children. Matty died of a heart attack in 1975 as he worked at one of his hobbies, gardening.

KEOSEY "GUY" BROWN

Winner of the Southern Middle and Light-heavyweight Championships in 1947 and 1948, Brown was known as "One Punch Guy Brown." Also known as a real "crowd pleaser," Brown was popular with most of the promoters and boxing commissions in Charlotte, Gastonia and Asheville. Possessing great physical stamina, he was booked somewhere in the Carolinas almost weekly in the mid-1940's. As one of the top middle and light-heavyweight boxers of the era, Brown was coached by the legendary Ebb Gantt. In 1948 he posted 28 consecutive wins. Through 1947 it was reported that Brown fought in 341, winning 277. His career tailed off in early 1950's

D.C. SMITH

Legendary manager and promotor, DC carved out many boxers in the forties and fifties and staged many bouts throughout the Carolinas. He had a knack for recognizing young and upcoming fighters during the most fertile boxing period in the Carolinas. He also designed some innovative training equipment.

THURMAN "CROW" PEELE

Peele, now living in Baton Rouge, La., was one of the three successful boxing brothers. Like many boxers, he began his amateur career in the Carolinas Golden Gloves tournament, winning the tournament in 1950-51-52-53. He also boxed in the National Golden Gloves Finals in New York City during this time. Peele attended the University of Louisiana and never lost a fight during his collegiate career. He won the NCAA Collegiate Boxing Championship in 1955. He turned professional after college and boxed several ranked heavyweights, including Joey Rowland and Charlie Norkus. While a professional, Peele served as a sparring partner with legendary light heavyweight champion Archie Moore. Peele's amateur record stands at an amazing 195-5 while his professional record boasts 37 wins and 2 losses.

NATHAN H. "KID" CROSBY

Born in Beaufort, S.C. on Sept. 29, 1919, Nathan "Kid" Crosby was a heavy puncher with a world of ring savvy. Beginning at a young age, Crosby was taught the sport of boxing by his father, himself the Southern Bantamweight champion at one time. Crosby, a welterweight, compiled a record of 151 wins against just four losses, with 87 of his wins via the KO route. Most of his matches were as a professional. He dodged no man, having fought the great Al Reid of Greenwood, S.C. who was one of the few boxers to score a knockdown of Sugar Ray Robinson. Crosby fought in the Greenville/Spartanburg area in the beginning of his career, and then moved to Texas where he was managed by Frankie Edwards, once the manager of Gene Tunney. Crosby defeated such fighters as Chino Lopez, Howard Steen, Paul Altman, Al Hamm, Joe Comforto, and Tommy Roman, all highly regarded professionals. Lopez, in fact, was named the world's best boxer by Ring Magazine in 1944.

After hanging up his gloves, Crosby became a minister in 1951. He pastored churches in Texas and did missionary work in Mexico until his retirement in 1979. Crosby passed away in 1985. His wife Helen and two daughters still live in Houston.

JACKIE NICK THEODORE

Posting an overall record of 56-1, Theodore made a quick impact when he began his career in 1956 at the age of 16. As a novice, he won every tournament to earn two Carolinas Lightweight Championships. Moving up to Welterweight division, Theodore continued his winning ways by earning three Carolinas Open Championships. In 1958 and 1959, he represented the Carolinas in the Eastern Golden Gloves Championships in New York's Madison Square Garden. In 1960, Theodore relocated to Florida and was drafted into the U.S. Army in 1966. There he resumed his boxing career winning the Welterweight Championship.

Still residing in North Miami Beach, Florida, he owns and operates a swimming pool contracting business.

OSCAR ELLINGTON

Ellington had the unique ability to parlay his success in the ring into a prominent position as an administrator for the sport of boxing. Fighting as an amateur from 1936-1941, Ellington earned the 1938 AAU North Carolina Boxing Championship in the 126-pound class. After hanging up his gloves, he served as president of the AAU boxing committee representing North and South Carolina for 42 years. He served as a committeeman for the XXVII CISM Boxing Championships in 1975. Highlighting a brilliant career as a sports administrator, Ellington served on the United States Olympic Boxing Team as a committeeman for the 1976 Olympics in Montreal. He was inducted into the United States Boxing Hall of Fame in 1980.

ARTHUR DAVIS

Arthur is the older brother of the famed Davis brothers of Mount Holly. Arthur, who later developed the boxing nickname of "Crash," began his illustrious boxing career at the young age of thirteen with the Mount Holly Boxing Team. Arthur emerged as a fast growing star by winning the N.C. Featherweight Division in 1943. After the Navy7, Arthur enrolled at N.C. State and resumed his boxing career, compiling a record 61 wins and 6 defeats.

Arthur began his professional boxing career in July 1949 under the management of Chris Dundee. After five years he retired after compiling a record of 40 wins, nine defeats and five draws.

After his professional boxing career, Arthur continued his second love of full-time teaching. After retiring as principal he and wife Edna returned home to North Carolina and settled in Hendersonville.

Regretfully, Arthur is no longer with us as he fought his toughest fight and lost to cancer.

WILLIAM "BILLUM" WILKINSON

Bill Wilkinson participated in the very first Carolinas Golden Gloves in Charlotte in 1933 and walked away with the bantamweight crown. He took the lightweight title in 1935. Wilkinson was unable to enter the Charlotte tournament again until 1939, but he again won the lightweight title that year. A native of Lincolnton, N.C. Wilkinson fought 125 times and lost just four bouts and was never knocked out. He attended King College in Bristol, Tenn. On a boxing scholarship, where one of his teammates was Ed Sweet, a member of the Carolinas Boxing Hall of Fame from Cornelius, N.C. Wilkinson was undefeated throughout his college career. Most of his fights were as a lightweight. He was recognized as smart ring general with good punching power in both hands. Wilkinson won Golden Gloves titles in Charlotte, Raleigh and High Point. He represented the state in a national tournament in Cleveland, where he dropped a close decision.

Wilkinson spent his working years as an executive with Coca Cola Co. in Bristol. He and his wife Elizabeth, now deceased, are the parents of three.

LACY HALL

The year 1949 was a good one for Burlington, N.C. welterweight Lacy Hall. He ran through all competition in his weight class, winning amateur tournaments in Burlington, Durham, High Point, and Greensboro. Before the year was up he had won 16 consecutive matches and he picked up three outstanding boxer trophies along the way.

Hall received undergraduate degrees from Elon College and Duke. He earned a masters and a Ph.D. from UNC Chapel Hill. Hall served in the U.S. Army for three years. He is past president and owner of King's Business College in Greensboro. Hall has been involved in many areas of community service over the years. He has also written books on business and mental health. He is cofounder and president of the Huck Finn Tennis Charity Fund.

He and his wife Barbara have one daughter. Hall lists writing, poetry, gardening, wine making, and traveling among his hobbies.

WOODY WOODCOCK

Born in Pelzer, S.C. in 1921, Woodcock began boxing at age 14 and won several amateur tournaments in the Upstate of South Carolina and Charlotte area. He joined the U.S. Army in 1939, and after being transferred to Panama, held the Panamanian lightweight amateur championship title in 1941 and 1942. Woodcock also captured the all-service championship in 1942. After turning professional in 1943, Woodcock fought the very best in his weight class on the way to becoming the number-one ranked featherweight. Woodcock retired from the ring in 1952 after compiling an overall record of 129 wins against only 12 losses, including an impressive 43 and five record as an amateur.

In retirement, Woodcock coached young boxers at The Citadel and refereed AAU bouts. He has been involved in boxing as a fighter, referee, coach, and official for 64 years and continues to judge professional bouts in Charleston.

Woodcock and his wife, Kit, reside in Summerville, S.C. where he is active in his church and community.

ALEXANDER WALTON AKA "BUCK EARNHARDT"

(Deceased)

Wife: Melba Lee Walton of Spartanburg, SC

Personal Data: Born: July 7, 1926 in Salisbury, NC. The son of George and Callie (Waller) Walton; raised by his aunt and uncle , Mr. & Mrs. T.C. Earnhardt.

Children: Five children – 3 Boys, 2 Girls, 10 Grandchildren and 8 Great- Grandchildren

Hobbies: Coaching

Buck enlisted in United STated Navy on March 9, 1944. On August 31, 1944 he is listed on board the USS Clyde. Then on April 1, 1946 he is listed amond the crew of the USS Unicoi as a Seaman 1st Class. Buck began his boxing career during his service in the Navy.Many of the results were not available. During this period of time, the newspapers focused on the War both in Europe and Pacific. Sports paged in the Spartanburg newspapers were usually one-page and devoted mostly to baseball. An article titled "Carl Chastain Heads Armory Fight Card Here- Boxes Buck Earnhardt in 19 Rounder" which appeared in the Spartanburg Herald Journal, state: "Buck Earnhardt has 40 triumphs, 21 setbacks and a pair of draws. He has floored 28 foes." Former boxers from this era estimate that Buck probably had about 100 professional fights.

By 1957, Buck had been boxing for over 10 years.

Awards: Buck coached with Henry "Pappy" Gault for the city of Spartanburg Boxing Team in the mid 1960's.

In 1963, Buck coached the Salvation Army Boys' Club Bantam League Football team to the city championship with an 8-0 record.

In 1964, Buck's Little League Baseball team the "Luncheon Optimist", posted a perfect 22-0 record to win the city championship. Several players from these teams went on to play college ball, with one player from this championship baseball team going on to play professional baseball.

Buck influenced a lot of young men's lives in the Spartan Mills community in and out of the rung. He retired from Southern Railway in 1990 after 40 years of service.

He passed in Spartanburg on September 29, 1994.

JAMES "BONECRUSHER" SMITH

When Bonecrusher Smith knocked out WBA heavyweight champion Tim Witherspoon in the first round in 1986, he became the first heavyweight champion with a college degree, having acquired a bachelor's degree in business administration from Shaw University. A native of Magnolia, N.C., Smith started boxing while serving in the U.S. Army. After leaving the military, he went to work with the North Carolina Department of Corrections. He began his professional career with a 1981 bout on ESPN, which he lost, but then he upset future cruiserweight Rickey Parker, followed by three more wins over respected opponents. Smith then scored nine straight knockout wins to gain a fight with undefeated British prospect Frank Bruno. To everyone's surprise he knocked out the favored Brit in the 10th round. In 1987, Smith risked his championship belt against Mike Tyson's WBC belt in Las Vegas, and he lost a decision. He fought off and on for several years winning most of his bouts by knockout. In 1999, Smith lost a decision to his friend Larry Holmes and at the age of 46 hung up his gloves. He compiled a record of 44-17-1 as a professional and won many amateur and military fights.

After retiring, Smith became an ordained minister and dedicated his life to helping young people stay clear of crime and drugs. He and his wife, Reba, are the parents of three.

For more information on Carolina boxer's go to

www.carolinaboxinghalloffame.com

At this time I would like to thank my wife Kay for all her hard work, love and support, without her dedication I could not have written this book. I also want to thank Susan Martin for her help with editing. And again I thank everyone so much for choosing my book to read. I hope you did like it and will tell a friend about Still Standing: After the Bell. Thank you again.

Sincerely,

Brent Hensley